Aftermath

Aftermath

an anthology

Edited by Gill James

Chapeltown Books

British Library Cataloguing in Publication Data

A Record of this Publication is available from the British Library

ISBN 978-1-910542-74-3

This edition published 2021 by Chapeltown Books
Manchester, England

Contents

Introduction

Aftermath is the companion book to *Covid 19: An Extraordinary Time*.

For both books we invited writers who are published by Bridge House, CaféLit, Chapeltown and The Red Telephone, and their trusted friends, to submit texts they created in 2020 whilst the world began to get used to and control Covid 19. All of the works here have been edited but only lightly.

We accepted all submitted pieces. This time we kept going until we had fifty texts. We've again arranged the works in date order so they reflect any changing mood. Only in order to accommodate a formatting issue such as having a poem on one double page spread instead of including a page turn have we deviated from this a little.

These are souvenir books. They are books writers may want to bury in a time capsule. You're probably reading this because you are or you know one of the contributing writers. This offers a partial record of a truly extraordinary time – hence our subtitle on the first book. We felt it needed documenting but not merely in descriptive prose, as Samuel Pepys did in his diaries, which describe some equally challenging times, but in all sorts of other texts, texts that show the creativity of their authors.

As I write this, the vaccine is rolling out and deaths and severe cases are dropping but new variants are emerging. We are returning to something that approaches normality but also holding on to some of the new things we've learnt. Hopefully this book also records some of those.

Gill James April 2021

When Corona Virus Leaves Town

Colin Payn

Isn't that what we all want? Yet numerous commentators are predicting that it will be a new normal we return to, whether it happens in a year or five years, they believe that we will all live in a changed world. Some are optimistic about our wakeup call on the environment, the cleaner air during lock down forcing recognition that we must never get back to a situation where more people are dying of pollution each year than the virus at its worst.[1]

Others believe, 'When life returns to normal…' that the nature of the pandemic will bring governments around the world to the stark realisation that it probably won't be the last, and the only way to avoid another health and economic catastrophe will be to work closer together.

Another cause for optimism may be that the first wave of the virus will be defeated in first world countries, and the fear of a second wave coming crashing in from countries with under developed health systems could lead to a transfer of wealth and expertise into those areas, purely out of self-interest.

At the top end of the optimism curve is the hope that a world order would emerge that recognises the interdependence of all countries, and leads to a rejection of armed conflict anywhere.

Sadly, there is, as yet, little evidence that any of these outcomes are the focus of world leaders. Quite the opposite. In countries where democracy is already weak their leaders have taken the opportunity to enhance their control of the population through

---

1 Air pollution deaths worldwide in 2017: 8 million. Source: Global Alliance on Health & Pollution.

Covid-19 deaths worldwide at 20th April 2020: 165,000. Source: European Centre for Disease Prevention and Control.

legislation and through technology.[2] Where close ties between mature democracies, such as within the EU, have existed for some time, there has been a knee jerk reaction to protect their economies and population on a national basis. Even within the far more integrated economy of the USA there has been a political factionalism, setting State against State and led by the President.

So, where does this leave the global economy as companies navigate their way out of the shutdown, aided or not by their Governments?

The big picture is that we are at the beginning of what has been called, the Fourth Industrial Revolution[3], a time when the most obvious take-over of jobs by machines has been in the manufacturing industry. The number of robots in use varies greatly by country, with the UK pretty much bottom of the developed world pile.[4] Which could account for the poor productivity record where labour is deemed more abundant than innovation.

But, when a manned production line has to be completely closed down because of the pandemic, whilst another can be kept working because there are few staff but many robots, then the economic case for commercial life returning to 'normal' will be harder to make. There will be many companies, not just in the UK but around the world, taking this opportunity to re-evaluate their business model.

However, the real Revolution is not even about industry, it is about the service sector. The professionals like solicitors, accountants, designers, surveyors, even in a cannibalistic way, the computer experts. Plus all their office staff. For all its over-hyped capability, the fact is Artificial Intelligence, even in its crude mass learning current state, is capable of being tasked to handle millions of jobs that are employing workers week in and week out.

---

[2] In Romania the Prime Minister has taken over full control; Egypt has revoked the rights of the Guardian's reporter for questioning their Covid -19 figures; Jordan has closed all news outlets; China, Brazil and Turkey have all seen citizen's rights reduced.

[3] The Fourth Industrial Revolution by Klaus Schwab.

[4] 21st out of 30 in 2017 according to the Information Technology Foundation.

You may ask why, if this is so, companies haven't installed AI already?

The answer may be in the risk averse culture of many professions, or it may be in the fact that the very managers who would be in a position to recommend AI to the Board are the ones who would lose their jobs if it was implemented.

It is likely that Covid-19 will persuade many service companies to investigate the possibilities, and some will take the chance to invest in systems that will enable them to offer the same services as before but without the high staff costs, including office rents and rates, or the danger of being closed down by another pandemic. Companies in this position will have the choice of undercutting rivals or taking greater profit. Either result would cause turbulence in their markets and be quickly followed by secondary adopters.

Scale this up to all world service and manufacturing industries and the effect would be enormous and probably, unsustainable levels of unemployment.

The Fourth Industrial Revolution is not a new concept, but evidence can be found in both industry and the professions that the use of AI is increasing. From the sight of linked, unmanned tractors ploughing thousands of acres at a time, to the legal systems able to locate previous case law in seconds rather than hours.

What Covid-19 may have done is push the accelerator harder for many companies, and even public bodies, in efforts to move away from the risks of relying on human employees in an age of heightened uncertainty. When the alternative of AI is becoming more widespread, the chances of 'life returning to normal' are pretty remote.

Dragonfly

Linda Morse

We larvae have lived and hunted alone for a long time now. Skulking in an existence of murky weed and pond mud. We have become sneaking predators, snatching whatever prey comes near our grasp. We have been hideous in our masks, with our claws extended, greedily snatching and devouring any small amount of life on offer. Making sure we have enough. More than enough.

Inexorable days and weeks pile up, along with the debris of our irritable, grudging lack of rebellion. The restless resentment builds and builds. We have eaten enough. We are bloated, over-extended. We want air, wings. We demand freedom. Flight. Each extra moment we are forced to cramp in this ugly, misshapen, larval body feels eternal. There seems no way out.

Ever.

This is my limit. My rupturing obesity can take no more. Release may be impossible, but still I attempt to crawl, heavily struggling to carry this grotesque carcass to the surface. I'll break the water's subtle skin. See the light I know exists.

Climb.

It is too hard. A voice is screaming within me, *Surrender. Surrender now and fall back into the familiar murk.* I know it will receive me softly and let me sink forever. Falling, circling, losing height, losing sense, I could sink into the gentle mud.

Effortless.

I see a stem. A reed. It is a fragile thing, such a fragile chance, but it thrills me. The weak and trivial thing glimmers, a dim beacon of freedom. With my final strength I grasp it. Haul myself up with every last fibre of my frame. Why am I expending my energy on this, when I could choose oblivion? Without an answer, I break through. At the moment of collapse, I am gifted the staggering brightness of light. I feel the zinging of air. Hear the screeching of the sky-diving harpies, who would take me in their beaks. They fill me with a terror. They fill me with determination to live. I am driven by a new vitality, a force pushing me upwards. Pushing me to climb and toil until I reach stillness.

Stop… Wait…. Sleep…?

Time… Slowly… Passes…

This is not torpor, not hesitation.

This is peace.

This is right.

The moment strikes.

Now.

Everything pushes, struggles, fights. All my body battles furiously against the restriction, the enclosure, the lockdown. My body fights like it has never fought before. My head bursts out of my skull, my brain is free.

Don't stop. Don't stop. Don't stop.

Then… rest once more.

Take breath… but never, never stop.

Even as the harpies swoop around me, taking others, taking my friends, I will not give up. There are thousands of us emerging, ecstatic and defenseless. Beaks circle. The shouting is deafening.

Don't stop.

Then the danger has moved on. I am rested. I can breathe! I can flex and expand, arch and stretch.

I can split open.

Unfold.

In a flash of blue and silver, in the sparkle on the water, in the far distance of those ghastly depths, I understand my reason for existence. Reflected in the pool, I stretch out unfamiliar, crushed and long-folded wings.

Wings.

I see that I am fabulous, blue and yellow, fine and sparkling.

Bigger.

So much bigger.

I was dormant and whilst I was lazy, green-brown and ugly, I matured…

became ready to fly.

The Lifeline

Dawn Knox

Come on! Come on! Lily held her breath.

The coloured disc spun in the middle of her screen as the computer struggled to open the program.

Money was tight since she'd been made redundant several months ago, nevertheless she'd just placed an order for a new high-powered laptop and the sooner it was delivered, the better. A working computer was absolutely crucial. It was Lily's link to the world.

Before her mother's premature death of COVID-19, she used to say, "The only necessities in this world are the food you eat, the home you live in and the clothes you wear. Everything else is a luxury." And perhaps that had been true once, but not these days. Lily needed the computer to order groceries and take-way meals; to find workmen to fix the dishwasher and the roof when it leaked and to browse the online shops for clothes. Not that she needed many new clothes. She rarely went out and it was mostly a question of replacing the comfortable and sloppy garments she wore daily.

Of course, it wasn't that she *couldn't* go out but why bother when most things could be done online? There had been restricted opening of restaurants, bars and hotels months before the stringent lockdown had finally been lifted but everyone knew the virus was still a threat. And until the entire world's population was immunised against the virus or it was eradicated, the shadow of disease and death hung over them still, despite encouragement from politicians to carry on whilst staying alert for risks.

The last time she'd been to a café with a friend, they'd bumped elbows then sat at an acceptable distance from each other and from other customers. Although it was mid-morning, the café had the air of an establishment which was about to close for the day, with mask-wearing baristas hovering attentively as if waiting for the few customers to leave, while they busied themselves, spraying tables and other common surfaces with virus-obliterating chemicals. There'd been no cheerful background babble interlaced with laughter nor the chink of spoon against cup and the clink of cup against saucer. Neither had there been smiling faces enjoying coffee and cake – just a handful of customers sliding masks to one side as they took a sip or bite and then covering their noses and mouths once more.

Lily had been on edge the entire time and had decided that before she resumed what had once passed as a social life, she'd wait until things got back to the way they'd been pre-lockdown, when no one flinched if a passer-by coughed or sneezed and nobody commented on the length of time others washed their hands in the public toilet.

Of course, there was the possibility that things would never revert to the way they'd been before *COVID-19* was on everyone's lips – especially if they'd touched their mouths with unwashed hands… Certainly, if things ever went back to normal, there'd be a long period of readjustment while people attempted to overcome the tendency to regard everyone they met as a harbinger of death. So, while Lily waited in self-isolation, her leisure time was spent participating in online lessons in yoga, ballet, cookery and anything else which took her fancy and going on virtual tours of online museums and art galleries.

Yes, the computer was a lifeline. It was essential to her mental wellbeing and in maintaining some sort of social life. After all, she didn't want to spend the rest of her days living on her own. For years she'd wanted to meet someone and share everything with him – although not the virus, of course.

Her antibody tests had repeatedly come back negative, so apparently, she was still vulnerable, and she wasn't sure how she'd cope on a real date. That was why it was so important her computer worked now. Her video meeting with Jake was due to take place in five minutes – but only if she could connect to the video conferencing platform.

The wheel continued to spin and with a sigh, she unlocked her phone. If she had to take the video call on a tiny screen, well, it would be better than nothing. As she considered rebooting the computer, the window suddenly opened and with a sigh of relief, she clicked on the video icon to start the camera. Her image appeared on the screen and she patted her hair into place, checked her lipstick and gave herself a hesitant smile.

At exactly seven o'clock, there was a ping and Jake appeared in another window next to hers. He smiled and waved at her.

"Hi there! How's your day been?" he asked as he winked at her.

Lily caught her breath. He was so handsome with the boyish, dark fringe that flopped forward when he became animated, and his intensely blue eyes framed with long, dark lashes. She watched his hands as he brushed the hair off his forehead. They were sensitive hands with long fingers. Artist's hands. *Beautiful* hands. A ripple of pleasure coursed through her. Everything about Jake was beautiful.

She told him about her day and he'd laughed when she showed him the burnt biscuits she'd forgotten to remove from the oven – his blue eyes crinkled at the corners and a lop-sided grin lit up his face… and gave *her* palpitations.

Jake told her about his day working from home, and later, when her father rang, Jake suggested Lily call him back when she'd finished talking to her dad – if she wanted.

She wanted. She definitely wanted.

Almost before her father said goodbye, she called Jake again and when he replied, they chatted easily – so easily, that although she hadn't intended to say anything, it felt so comfortable confiding in him how desperate she'd been feeling about having no job and how lonely she found it, living alone. Eventually, she said she'd better go and he suggested they talk again the following evening.

"Or earlier if you prefer," he said. "If you need to talk, I'm here."

As she curled up in bed, she felt calmer than she'd done all day. This new relationship was growing and blossoming each time they 'met'.

Thank God for my computer, she thought as she drifted off to sleep. Because without it, she wouldn't have come across the dating website and wouldn't have found Jake. He displayed sufficient interest in her without appearing to be overinvested and intrusive, his body language told her he was completely engaged with whatever she said and his expression as he'd blown her a kiss when they'd signed off had hinted that if they'd been together, in reality, he might have held her close and…

She shivered, unsure if it was a shudder of fear at the thought of irresponsible close contact or a quiver of pleasure at the prospect of such intimacy.

He liked her, she was sure and he completely understood her.

Well, most of the time, anyway.

She smiled as she remembered earlier that evening when she'd related an incident which had taken place some time ago at work and she'd described her boss as being like *a fish out of water.*

"She died?" Jake asked with a sympathetic expression, "I'm sorry to hear that."

"No, she didn't die," Lily had replied quickly, wondering what she'd said for him to misunderstand.

"But fish die when they're out of water," he'd said.

"Yes, but…" And then Lily had realised and had explained it was an idiom.

Jake had merely nodded and said, "I understand. So, carry on, what happened then?"

And she'd finished the story.

There would probably be more incidents like that, Lily acknowledged. After all, artificial intelligence had made significant advances recently and by the time she saw Jake again, he'd undoubtedly have assimilated every idiom known to man and their various nuances.

Physically, he was perfect but then virtual reality was quite sophisticated and when she'd signed up to the Virtual Partners dating site, she'd given detailed specifications of her ideal man. Jake matched them exactly.

He wasn't faultless *yet*.

But give him time.

He would be.

The Protecting Shadow of the Ancestors

Cath Barton

In here there is dark and there is darker. When the tone shifts into a higher key I mark the wall with my chalk. I do not attempt a tally. What I see is an emerging pattern, a scene that shifts and swirls. It is a kind of consolation, that moving picture in which I can conjure something beyond.

I was allowed to bring just two other things into this confinement. Knowing memory would be fugitive, I brought a photograph of you, a portrait of your smile. And a sprig of lavender, the sun-infused essence of Provence, a place of past happiness. The scent is fading, as the chalk wears down and some kind of change approaches.

I have been offered choices daily, on a menu printed out on paper like linen, which, afterwards, I fold into birds. I dream of their flight and, indeed, sometimes they have moved by morning, settled in a new formation. Lifted by unseen hands, I like to think.

And the things I choose each day, the food and the wine? At first I thought they would help, these rich tastes, succulence, smoothness. But the satisfactions are transitory. I am left, as darkness deepens, covered by a spreading blankness in which sleep is, like all else, a thing broken.

And now they have told me I can leave. The light through the open door hurts my eyes, shrunken now deep in my skull. For some time I stay, reluctant to take the necessary steps. But the paper birds fly out, carried by the fresh currents of air, and I know I have no option but to follow. Only after I have gone through the door and it has swung shut behind me with a dull thud do I realise that I have left behind the photograph, curled now, but still a representation of you and all we shared. I turn but there is no longer an opening. There is no option but to face the future.

I am walking, now, across the hot stones of the courtyard. The soft slap of my slippers echoes off the walls. Ahead of me is another door and the shadow of someone who is beckoning to me, calling me into the humid warmth of the silkworm chamber. It will be dark there too, but it will cocoon me. That, at least, is my hope.

Lockdown Losers

Roger Noons

We have heard a lot about big businesses and how they have been affected by the Pandemic, but what about the smaller enterprises, how are they fairing?

1. Miriam's

"Is that Mercian Loans?"

"Yes, how can I help you today?"

"My name's Miriam and I gather you operate the Coronavirus Business Interruption Loan Scheme on behalf of the Government?"

"Yes, we do. Are you a small business?"

"Yes."

"And the nature of your enterprise?"

"Massage."

"Pardon?"

"Miriam's Massage for Discerning Gentlemen."

"And you'd like a loan?"

"Yes please, ten thousand pounds will do."

"I'll have to ask my Line Manager, it may…"

"What's his name?"

"Mr Richard-Watt."

"Is that Willie Richard-Watt?"

"Er… yes, do you—"

"Please tell Willie that as he and his staff make up 70% of my clientele, I could do with the cash smartish… please."

2. Lenny the Loo

"How's it going, Lenny?"

"Lousy, Mate, they've closed the toilets in both car parks."

"Have you been furloughed?"

"No, I'm not an employee. I took on the franchise. I keep them clean, provide toilet paper and stuff and pay them fifty quid a week. I keep the money from the doors."

"Do yer make much?"

"I do at weekends, Christmas and when the sales are on. You'd be surprised how many women'll pay fifty pence for a pee."

"Well, if you've nothing to do—"

"I have to go, my job to clean up. Folks are squatting all over the place. It's disgusting. I'm there all day and getting nothing out of it. Although, one woman gave me a pound 'cause I stood watch while she was in a corner space."

"P'raps you should watch that space."

"Ha ha."

3. Freddie the Fix

"Got a problem, Boss?"

"Yeah and I need your help."

"You know I'll always do whatever I can. In fact I thought everything was hunky dory?"

"It's not. Business is hopeless. I've got loads of product, God knows how many customers and no delivery system."

"I thought—"

"Your idea of sending the stuff by Royal Mail labelled *Covid 19 samples for analysis* worked for three days, because you put 'em all in the same post box. Now they've got a sniffer dog in the Sorting Office."

"Right, so what now?"

"I want you to round up some of your mates, two or three, dwarfs—"

"Little people, Boss, we're—"

"Yeah, whatever, I've ordered kids bikes and I want you **little people**, to get kitted out. Trainers, jeans, anoraks and crash helmets. I'm having bags made with Express and Post on the side. You'll work early morning and teatime. Okay?"

"What about the papers?"

"What papers?"

"It might look better if we have one or two papers in the bags."

"Yeah, you're right. I'll sort that. Get your mates organised as soon as possible."

"About pay?"

"Two pounds a package, that do?"
"Can we keep the bikes?"

4. Billy the... Pilferer

"What's up Bill?"

"It's hopeless Luv, terrible. Nobody's leaving their house. Doors shut and locked, alarms switched on. One house put out an old ironing board and a rusty kettle. When I picked it up, the 'andle came off in me 'and. I don't know what I'm goin' to do. The bloody clothes aid people are doing a bomb 'cause women are at 'ome all day clearing out drawers and wardrobes, buying *their new outfits for when it's all over,* on their computers."

"What about the Government's Scheme?"

"That's bound to be a winner, Wend. And what is your profession, Mr Wilde? Burglar, I see and how much do you usually make a week?"

"We'll manage, don't you fret." She sniggered. "I can always stand under the Town Clock."

"Are your arms two metres long?"

Closure

Vanessa Horn

Tom forced a smile as he entered the lounge and passed his flatmate a beer. "Anything?"

Luke switched off the TV before taking the can. "Cheers mate. Nope, no news. Just the usual loop of comedy repeats."

"I wonder…" Tom stopped, not knowing how to finish the sentence.

But Luke seemed to know. "Yeah." Then he lowered his voice. "Have you looked out today?"

Tom shook his head. "Too risky in daylight. I will tonight. But… there's something more important: food stocks are getting low. I reckon we've only got enough for another two weeks, even if we eke them out. And… maybe four weeks of generator fuel."

Luke stared. "Then what?"

Tom sighed. "They'll have to replenish our stocks – they can't expect us to starve to death."

"But no-one would be allow…" Luke's voice petered out but then he brightened. "Yeah, they've probably relaxed the rules by now – it's been such a long time. And… maybe the virus has burnt itself out?"

Tom frowned. "Though… wouldn't you think we'd have been told? Or at least heard people outside again?"

Luke shook his head. "God knows. If only the Internet was still up and running." Then he grinned. "But there'll be plenty of people in the same situation as us – everyone had the same rations allotted when lockdown started. So, there'll be something organised. Some sort of plan."

"Yeah." Tom hoped he sounded more convincing than he felt. "Bound to be."

That evening Tom waited until he was sure it would be dark outside and then switched off the living room light. Kneeling by the closed curtains, his hands shaking as was normal when he did this, he peered out of the tiny gap which they'd – illegally – left open. Having that little chink of hope had made the two of them feel less isolated during the past months, knowing that other people were not too far away. It had been a comfort. A support. But now, just as for the last two weeks, when he stared outside there was no sign of life. Just dark houses, unlit streetlamps, empty roads.

Tom sighed. He hadn't realised how much seeing evidence of humanity, albeit just flickers of light and shadows, had comforted him. It, he supposed, just a reminder that people were around, going about their lives, even though only indoors. Luke, too, although he refused to break the rules by looking out himself, relied on Tom to talk to him about the sightings. The reassurances. But now… nothing. What should he say to Luke? Though, was there really anything to say, beyond the fact that he couldn't see anything? Anyone. No signs didn't necessarily mean that people weren't still there. Did it?

He stood up quickly, flicking the light switch back on. No point in worrying unnecessarily. The government wouldn't let them down.

Nearly three weeks later, though, Tom's optimism was waning. There'd still been no sign of food stocks being replenished, or even a message about any procedures which needed to be followed. Now, all that was left in the flat were two vats of water and a few biscuits. He sat in front of the comedy repeats on the TV, formulating – and then discarding – possible explanations and solutions in his mind. Was it time to act?

He looked up as Luke came into the room. His friend had an odd expression on his face. Determination? Belligerence? Tom wasn't sure, but he'd rarely seen Luke look like that before.

Luke's voice was resolute. "I'm going to get us some food."

Tom gaped. "But…" he began, hearing his voice waver, even though Luke's plan was one he'd considered only minutes ago. But it was just a thought. He tried again, assuming an assertiveness he didn't feel. "Is that wise?"

Luke snorted. "What choice is there? It's obvious that no-one is coming to help us. This way at least I'll be doing something positive."

"And what if you get caught?" said Tom. "You could be sent to prison… or worse."

Luke shrugged. "At least in prison I'd get fed." Then he laughed. "And have a few more faces to look at than your ugly mug day in day out." He put on his jacket. "I won't be long…"

It seemed like ages since Luke had left the flat, even though Tom calculated it couldn't have been more than an hour. Immediately after his friend had gone, he wished he'd insisted on accompanying him; even being out and exposed to the virus or the police was surely better than sitting around waiting? But, as Luke had reminded him, there was no point in them both taking the risk. Nevertheless, Tom's thoughts whirled and swirled with worst-case scenarios. Suppose Luke was caught out and taken off to prison? Suppose he became infected with the virus; would he be admitted to hospital or were they still stating that infected people had to stay at home? Suppose… Tom sighed, trying to calm his mind and straining his ears for any sound of his friend returning.

When, finally, Tom heard the key in the lock, he leapt up, running to the front door, his heart pounding erratically.

At first glance, Luke looked much the same as he had when he'd left – just, possibly, a little paler. But – thank God – there were no officials with him, *and* he had a bulging carrier bag slung over his shoulder. Seeing Tom's eyes drawn to this, he nodded. "I managed to break into the supermarket on the main street – got a few cans and things that hadn't gone out of date."

"You broke in?" said Tom, blinking. "But why was it closed?"

Luke placed the bag on the floor. "Everything's closed, mate – it's deserted out there. I walked for miles, trying to find someone – *anyone* – who I could ask what's going on but there was no-one a—" he stopped suddenly and looked down, his shoulders hunched. Muttered, "And the smell…"

Tom frowned. What smell? What was his friend not telling

him? Then, suddenly, the realisation hit him. He stared at Luke, feeling his heart racing to the point where he felt it would explode. “You don’t mean…?” No, it wasn’t possible. Couldn’t be.

Luke looked up again. “Yes. We’re the only ones alive.”

Leaving

Vanessa Horn

Amy watched as the sunlight sparkled through the window, highlighting the dancing dust motes. Was today the day? She closed her eyes, feeling the warmth on her face. I could do it today, she thought, surprising herself. If I had to choose a day, it could be today. Then she shivered and opened her eyes, her fleeting courage gone. If only it were that easy. Yet… why not? Why not today?

Now, suddenly emboldened, she rose from the chair and slowly walked the ten steps to the door. She stared down the hallway. If she chose to do it, there were another eleven steps to be walked to the front door. The entrance. The *exit*. Gazing at the shiny handle, she imagined it being pushed down. The door opening. Simple.

Opportunities: they were outside. The things that she used to do… before. Life would get back to, well, some sort of normality, she presumed. Other people had spanned this bridge over the past few weeks – she'd seen them pass by her windows, chatting, smiling – so she knew it could be done. But… had they been too quick in believing the authorities when they said it was safe to go out? *Was* it safe?

Excuses. It was so easy to find them. To be controlled by them. No, she had to do it. Now. Amy took one, then another step towards the door, feeling her heartbeat accelerate with every pace. Okay… focus on the benefits: visiting friends… walking in the sun… Another step… another… a few more…

Trembling, she reached out and touched the door handle. It was cool and solid – something you could rely on. Was she ready? Yes: she *had* to be. Before she could change her mind, she took a deep breath and pushed the handle down…

Paradise

Jim Bates

My wife and I were sitting in the living room reading and taking frequents breaks to check our phones to see what the recent news was with Covid-19. It was the beginning of the fourth week of the state imposed lock down and it already felt we'd been doing this for a year. We were gearing up for a long haul.

Suddenly Emily looked at me and frowned. I met her gaze, "What?"

"Bad news," she said, grimacing.

It seemed like we were spending every minute of every day hearing about and talking about the pandemic. Bad news was becoming a way of life. "Someone we know have the virus?" I asked, my heart rate speeding up.

"Sort of. John Prine died."

"Damn it," I spat out. "I thought he might make it."

We'd read the week before that he'd been infected. He'd been in poor health recently, but still… he was only seventy-three, my age. I loved him as singer songwriter and was sad to hear he'd passed on.

Emily shook her head. "Me, too." She was quiet for a minute before saying, "He'd been in the ICU for eight days."

"Shit," I said, angry at the circumstances causing his death.

But then a song of his came into my head, *Paradise*, and I started to mellow out, suddenly at a loss for words, remembering the first time I'd heard his music. It seemed like it was only yesterday…

The year was 1971. I had returned from Vietnam in January and was working that summer as a dishwasher at Ken's Café on the University of Minnesota campus. I'd just gotten back to the apartment after a ten hour shift and was sprawled on the couch smoking a joint when Tim walked in.

He held up a shopping bag. "Check this out."

"What have you got?" I took a hit and offered it to him. He took a deep drag and held it in. "John Prine's first album," he said exhaling and coughing a little. "It just came out."

He put it on the turn table and, given what we were doing at that very moment, we were hooked by the first song, *Illegal Smile*. We listened to the album about ten times that night, smoking and talking, digging the music and the words to his songs. We became immediate fans. So did our other two roommates, and it became a pattern that summer: coming home from work, smoking our dope and listening to John Prine. I even figured out the chords to the fifth song on the album, *Paradise,* and Tim and I sang it together sometimes while I played guitar. It was a memorable summer.

But then life got in the way. Early the next year Tim was convicted for resisting the draft and was sent to prison in Missouri. I drove down to visit him a few times but tapered off after I started going to college. We eventually lost touch. I heard later that he'd stayed in Missouri after he was released, met a woman named Sunshine and moved to a commune south of Eugene, Oregon.

I finished college with a degree in education and started teaching science in the Minneapolis school system. A few years later I met Emily while we were both working weekends at the North Country Coop. We married and built a life together, living in an older section of Minneapolis and raising three kids. I taught high school biology and Emily was a stay-at-home mom who also worked as a self-employed seamstress. It was a good life, and we had no reason to think we wouldn't be able to live it out to the end of our days the way nature intended. But it turned out nature had other plans in the name of Covid-19.

That night, after we heard the news about John Prine's death, we both went silent for a while. Emily had listened to his first album with her roommates when she'd gone to college and had wonderful memories of those times, much like me and Tim and our friends. The two of us listened to it when we first started dating, sharing a blossoming love for each other as well as John's music, which became sort of a corner stone for our relationship.

After a while, Emily got up, crossed the living room and hugged me. “We still have his album around here somewhere?”

That old album had long since bit the dust. “Remember? It was pretty beat up,” I told her. “I had to replace it with a CD. It’s downstairs.”

“Why don’t you try and find it?” she said and kissed me again.

I went down to my workroom and rifled through my stash of albums and CDs. It didn’t take long to put my hands on what I was looking for and I hurried back upstairs, holding the scratched jewel case out for her to see. “Found it.”

Emily’s bright smile took away some of my sadness. She still made me happy just by being around her. “Let’s have a listen.”

“Sure. You bet.”

We had a little boom box under an end table in the far corner of the living room. I put the CD in, started it and joined Emily on the couch. We listened all the way through, both of us quiet, lost in our memories of way back then.

When it was over, she ran her fingers through my hair and asked, “Didn’t you used to play that song, *Paradise*?”

I grinned. “Yeah, but not very good.”

“Do you think you could you play it now?”

I knew what she was asking. She was asking if we could go back to those earlier years when life was simpler and we were first falling in love and didn’t even begin to think about something like a pandemic and the possibility of people we knew dying.

“Sure,” I said. “I’ll be back in a minute.”

I went downstairs and got out my old martin, tuned it and brought it back to her. I played the song while Emily listened and hummed along,

Daddy won’t you take me back to Muhlenberg County, down by the Green River where Paradise lay.
I’m sorry my son but you’re too late in asking. Mr. Peabody’s coal train has hauled it away.

Then I played it again.

“Thanks,” she said when I finished. “That was nice.”

I went downstairs and put my guitar away. When I came back she was on the phone. "Who are you talking to?" I asked.

She covered the mouthpiece. "Jason." We talked to our kids every day, now that the pandemic was so prevalent.

"Let me talk to him when you're done." Jason was our oldest son.

And she did. In fact, we talked to all three of our kids that night, and our grandchildren, too, giving everyone in our family our love and best wishes for them to be safe and well. It seemed like the right thing to do.

There was a pandemic going on and people were dying. We were all trying to survive. I felt that if John Prine was alive he might have done the same thing, call his family and tell them he loved them, maybe even write a song about it. It might have been a little thing, but it made perfect sense. And coming from him, that song would have helped make things a little less crazy. In fact, I'm sure of it.

When we were doing talking on the phone I went back downstairs and got John's CD, thinking that we might want to listen to it again. I grabbed my guitar too, just in case. This pandemic wasn't going away anytime soon. A little music might help.

Walking and Talking

Jim Bates

For years I've taken a walk every morning in our small town. There's a trail along a roadway near where I live and I love getting out and enjoying a bit of fresh air, especially now when winter is losing its icy grip and springtime is fast approaching. In the past few weeks the snow has melted away completely and the lakes have lost their covering of ice and opened up. It's delightful being outside. I even heard a song sparrow singing the other day.

Most days I'd see a only a handful of people. We'd rarely greet, preferring, instead, to pass on by with our heads down, ignoring each other and carrying our special solitude deep inside. Then Covid-19 reared its ugly head: people getting sick, people dying, not enough medical supplies to go around and a president who had no empathy for the situation whatsoever. Then came Lock Down. Traffic dwindled to the bare minimum, people were warned to stay inside, and, if they did go out, to maintain a safe social distance. Life went on but in a different way as we all learned to adjust.

These days I still go for my walk, but I've noticed something has changed: more people are out walking than ever before. And, as opposed to the rather perfunctory nod like in the past, they are giving out a friendly wave, as if to say, *We're all in this together. Take care*. (While maintaining a respectable social distance, of course.) It's nice to see. Also, people are spending more time in their yards, having parked their cars for the foreseeable future. The truth of the matter is that folks are taking it upon themselves to get used to being at home. Life has slowed down and become more family orientated. Distance learning is in place now for the kids as parents become teachers.

Today, while walking by my neighbour's house, she looked up from raking her lawn, brushed a wisp of hair from her forehead and said, being friendly, "We're taking a recess. Thank goodness the weather's nice so the kids can play outside."

She pointed. Her young boy and girl were playing on a front yard swing set. I waved to them and they waved back. I turned to my neighbour. “So, how are you doing?” I asked, keeping six feet away.

“Good,” she said. “It’s hard. An adjustment. I miss my job, but the kids love having me home.”

“That sounds like a good thing,” I said.

She smiled. “Yeah. It is.”

We said good bye and I continued my walk. A flock of robins up ahead fluttered away from a puddle of water they’d been drinking from. A mother and father and their three kids rode by on their bikes. They smiled and waved. I waved back, thinking, maybe we’ll all be better neighbours to each other when all this is over. Better human beings.

When I got home I washed my hands and then called my son and two grandchildren. I used to see them every week but that was before the pandemic. I missed them and it was wonderful to hear their voices. We talked for a while until the kids had to leave. “We love you,” they said.

“I love you, too,” I told them, not wanting them to go.

And, at that very moment, in spite of all the horror and uncertainly of the future, just the sound of my loved ones voices and knowing they were well and safe, made everything all right.

“I’ll call you every day,” I told my son.

“That’ll be good, Dad,” he said. “I’d like that.” He paused. “Well, good bye.”

“Good bye.”

I sat and stared into space, thinking, before deciding what to do: I’d make a pact with myself. I would stay positive because tomorrow was another day. And another walk. More people to greet. And now, a special phone call to make.

Yes, that was as good a way as I could think of to get through this. I smiled, already looking forward to tomorrow. Then I sealed my pact with love.

Social Distancing

Jim Bates

Social distancing brought us together. It was the seventh week of lockdown and the governor had eased back on state imposed restrictions about being in public places so I took him up on it. My favourite coffee shop was open for walk-in traffic and take out and I decided to treat myself to a steaming latte.

It felt good to stroll the three blocks from my apartment and even better to open the door of Carl's Coffee and get smacked in the face with that roasted coffee bean aroma. Ah, it had been too long. Almost swooning, I moved into line.

"Hey, buddy!" A zealous manager suddenly appeared. "Six feet, remember?" He pointed to signs on the walls explaining the rule about not getting too close to anyone. In my excitement for being out in the world I'd forgotten and chastised myself for not remembering the drill. Should I make a joke and play my septuagenarian age card with him? No, better not. Why push it?

He pointed to brightly coloured orange circles on the floor with Six Feet written on them just to make his point, a picture being worth a thousand words, as they said. Point made. I got it.

"Sorry," I said, turning a little red. People were starting to stare. I stepped back quickly and bumped into a tiny woman who squeaked out an "Ouch" when I stepped on her foot. This was getting ridiculous. You'd think after being stuck inside for only seven weeks I'd at least remember how to act in public. But this was pandemic time and things were changing. Still…

I turned to her as I moved back to the required distance. "I'm so sorry. I don't know what's come over me."

Gray hair fluffed out over the collar of a jean jacket put her in the vicinity of my age. I could tell she was smiling because her eyes were twinkling behind her floral mask. "That's okay," she said, then quickly, and, as far as I was concerned, thankfully, changed the subject. "Do you live around here?" she asked. I was immediately impressed that she didn't get on my case for not wearing a face covering, or berate me for clumsily invading her space, not to mention potentially injuring her foot.

"I do. I live just a few blocks over," I said, pointing arbitrarily behind me.

"That's nice," she said. "I'm in town staying with my daughter."

We chatted as the line moved forward, keeping out distance, of course. She told me she was from New York City.

"Oh, my goodness, did you fly?" I was shocked. Getting on a plane at a time like this with Covid-19 running rampant seemed like an insane thing to do.

She smiled. "No. Well, yes," she laughed, understanding where I was coming from. "I flew in a few months ago, before the troubles (as she put it) began."

When we got to the counter I turned to her. "What are you having?" After a brief back-and-forth semi argument, she said, "Well, thank you. I'll have a latte."

Hmm. Same as me. "Two lattes, please." While the coffees were being made, I had an idea. "Say, would you like to join me?" I pointed outside. "It's a nice day. For Minnesota in the springtime, anyway. They've got their tables set up."

"Sure," she said. "That would be lovely."

I paid for our lattes and we took them outdoors. The morning sun was shining brightly warming the day and it felt good to be in the fresh air. We found two tables so we could sit six feet apart and continued chatting away and getting to get to know one another. It turned out we had a lot in common: we both liked to read, go for walks, cook and spend time with our grandchildren.

During a lull in our conversation, I said, "I don't mean to be too forward, but I'm having a wonderful time." She looked at me, raised her mask and took a sip of her latte, then replaced it. She seemed to be waiting for me to continue, so I did. "I was wondering if you'd like to meet again tomorrow." Her non-committal look worried me. I was enjoying being with her and hoped she felt the same way. "Right here. For coffee," I added, just to be clear. Was she interested? She was witty and charming and it had been years since I'll felt so comfortable with a woman. "I'll even pop for a scone."

She eyes crinkled as she laughed. "Well, if that's the case, how could I refuse?"

Whew! Relief flooded over me. "That's great," I grinned. Suddenly, the pandemic was starting to feel not quite so brutal.

"There's only one thing, though," she said, as her daughter pulled up to the curb and beeped her horn.

"What's that?" I asked, standing along with her, wondering if I'd missed something and offended her somehow.

"Could you please wear a mask tomorrow when we get together? I'd appreciate it." She pointed. All around everyone was masked up.

"Absolutely," I said, embarrassed. "I should have known better."

"Good," she said. "I'll see you tomorrow then, same time, same place."

She smiled, her lower face still covered. I waved good bye as she drove off with her daughter.

One of these days, hopefully, soon, I'll be able to see that smile of hers. In fact, as I began walking back to my apartment I found myself looking forward more and more to spending time with her. Her name was Sue. Maybe we'll be able to ride out the pandemic together and eventually not have to worry about masks and social distancing. One of these days the restrictions will be lifted and she'll be able to take her mask off. I'd love to be there when she does. I'll bet her smile is beautiful.

Bingley High Street During the Lockdown

Alyson Faye

Empty spaces stretch to eat up the town
where once forests of cars grew and took root
as traffic wardens strolled, on high alert
in their hi-vis armour;
brave and bold, I park horizontal across
three bays by the silenced Arts Centre.
Blinded cafés, nestle next to shuttered shops
and shock of shocks! No Wetherspoons,
with all its clamour and gaggles of
fag smokers outside -it's defunct, extinct;
the scattered cigarette ends lying
brownly on the pavement.

Forty years fade away, as I recall,
my 1977 on a Sunday,
brought back to life in 2020.
A flicker of movement on the bench-
an old man sits stroking a black cat,
flat cap and all.
In this changed town they are the same.
That bench, that bloke and that black cat.
I feel the pressure in my chest lift.
And I breathe.

Please read this last note after you've read the poem. Thanks

The black cat does not belong to the old man, nor vice versa; Apparently the cat has a home to go to but chooses to live out its life in the empty space next to the stocks by the Art Centre. The local vets are sick to death of it being brought in as a rescue. The vets didn't comment on the status of the old man but I am hoping he has a home too.

Remapping Me

Alyson Faye

An urban girl at heart
cafés, shops and galleries
my chosen habitats,
online and artisan my preferences
four wheels not two feet
take-out bread and cake
not home-baked.

A metropolitan butterfly
with her wings clipped.
As the cities shut up shop,
the neon signs wink out.
The terrain shifts -
green spaces beckon,
the woods welcome.

Daily I plunge, infiltrate
the trees' closed ranks,
hear the boughs sigh and roar,
absorbs the earthy tones,
maps the wreckage of a
murdered tree, its skeletal roots
reaching for the sky.
Trace the moss maps
and trail miles of choking ivy.

A skein of geese honk high above,
skimming the treetops.
Inside me, the space I've carved out,
grows, as perched, and grounded
I sit and see.

Resolute

Amanda Jones

What did we learn? Once the population had been reduced significantly the virus seemed to disappear. Was that its purpose? A mere few left in each country. All but a few survived.

Zoom had become one meeting every day for the remaining. It was 3pm in London and Catherine prepared. At first she slipped a smart top over her pyjamas then brushed her hair back, ragged at the edges and applied a little make-up.

Video was on. Audio connected. Then one by one the core forty appeared in their boxes and she swiped them left to right, right to left, left to right. The host, James, unmuted them all and a rush of talking battled its way from each box to reach someone, if only someone. Nobody was given the right to speak individually and Catherine could see people frantically listening out for a message. She looked for Lisa. Chat was switched off, messaging unavailable. James was the only one to dictate.

She found her. Right at the end of her left to right. Lisa was being clever. When Catherine waved with her forefinger tucked under Lisa held up a card. 'Resolute. 8pm. DuckDuckGo.' Just as she saw it and memorised it, scribbled it down, Lisa disappeared.

James was frowning, muted them all and began. A slideshow was shared and the usual statistics read out. How many born, how many living in the community, the S rating (likelihood of meeting a partner to reproduce x the distance from your Facebook location) and the coloured graphs showing what might happen if they did not go out, with transport, sports, skeleton supply shops etc.

Catherine changed her headset to music and was glad to end the meeting.

She found Lisa later online and they were able to have a proper chat. Lisa was the only other person she connected with in England, from Manchester. They arranged to meet.

The train took the HS2 route in its stride. Catherine watched the landscape in blinks and was the only one in the carriage. She saw three socially distanced people in the next one when boarding. It was safe enough.

Lisa stood by the barrier when she disembarked in Manchester. They hugged and held each other. It was recommended to do this whenever possible for mental health and they felt the endorphins relax them both. It was rare to meet someone to hold.

Taking a seat on a bench outside the station Lisa produced a folder. It was full of handwritten notes, divided into sections and with post-its sticking out.

"For this job you never use any computer. No device. Nothing. It must be handwritten. Read it all, follow the instructions and we'll meet again every week at a different station. See you online for the arrangement, same time."

Catherine nodded and they hugged again. Farewell holding was a recommended ten minutes and they took the time to whisper small talk, catching up on happenings and suchlike. Then Lisa left and Catherine boarded the next train back to London.

The Beach Where He Found It

Anne Goodwin

It was autumn when my daughter died. Yellowed leaves had shrouded her crumpled corpse by the time they found her in the grass verge between the pavement and the park. According to the coroner, it was the sludge of fallen leaves that killed her, made her slip and bang her head in the panic of attack; mugged for fifty quid and her mobile phone.

Some thought me brave, others thought me cold, the way I kept going, but I was neither. Forty-nine and no longer a mother, I clung to the old routines by the tips of my lacquered nails. I knew how to set the alarm and totter in heels to the bus stop. I knew how to operate a till. I'd already learnt to cook for one but I'd never adapt to a world without her.

A family of two since she was a toddler, it was a wrench when she moved out. But I was glad to step back and let her navigate her own life. I lapped up the airbrushed anecdotes she fed me over kitchen-table chats in our dressing gowns at Christmas and birthdays. After her death the changing seasons had no meaning: even on the brightest day, grey clouds choked the sun.

When I heard the message on the answerphone, I thought I'd gone crazy. It was a Thursday, the one night I worked late. I was tired, more tired than usual, although not tired enough to hallucinate. I played it through a dozen times and then I sat on the sofa, still in my coat, still in my heels, staring at nothing.

The voice was a stranger's but the words were hers. My mind panned through the possibilities, the glimmers of hope amongst the dread. Her death had been an elaborate charade to escape me. The police had her on witness protection. She was on the run with a man with a dubious past. Her long-lost father had claimed her; she'd been kidnapped and I had twenty-four hours to raise the ransom. Anything would do, so long as it meant it wasn't my daughter's body beneath that blanket of autumn leaves.

I listened again. The voice was jaunty: "I found your postcard. Let me know if you want it back." Then, as if reading from a script, my daughter's words.

A caravan perched above chalky cliffs, a picnic among the dunes. Still young enough to shape the sand into fairy-tale castles, yet old enough to battle the stove to bring me morning tea in bed. An imaginative child, romantic, she fancied she saw porpoises cresting the waves.

It was Miranda's idea to rinse out a fat-necked smoothie bottle and post her message through the waves. She swapped her pocket money at the on-site shop for a selection of picture postcards and a ballpoint with multi-coloured inks. She spent an entire rainy afternoon figuring what to write.

"I hope a Chinese lady finds it," she said.

I suspected it wouldn't make it as far as the next bay, but she could fantasise. "If you include our address she can write and let you know."

"And our phone number," she said. "So she can ring us up."

Perhaps it was out of apathy that I'd kept the landline. Perhaps I was also a dreamer, waiting for some faraway stranger to resurrect my child. The voice on my answerphone was male, however, and Scottish, but definitely quoting Miranda's words.

If this card should chance to roam
Please be kind and help it home.

He'd sent it on the first stage of its journey. Now it was up to me. I shed my coat, slipped off my shoes and picked up the phone.

It was a while before I was well enough to trek up to Scotland. Ian had offered to put the bottle in the post, but I couldn't risk losing her again. Besides, I needed to stand on the beach where he'd found it. I owed it to the memory of that holiday, to the girl who'd lent her optimism to the sea.

I'd put on weight in those weeks I was on sick leave, languishing on the sofa, stuffing my face with chocolate while staring at terrible TV. I slept through the alarm, or forgot to set it. I didn't have the energy to varnish my nails. I was pleased my daughter's message had reached dry land, yet it was as if they'd discovered her leaf-strewn body all over again.

Ian sounded amused when I first rang him, but he couldn't apologise enough when I explained. Even dismayed, his voice was soothing, the type of accent you'd want on the end of a helpline, promising to fix the problem, and soon.

I must have looked a fright in my frumpy cagoule and flatties when he met me at the station, but Ian was too much of a gentleman to let it show. He drove me to the beach, handed me the bottle, pointed out the café in the distance where he'd wait.

I'd imagined tramping along the shoreline, collecting shells and bits of jetsam to build a shrine. I'd imagined sobbing, collapsing, scrubbing sand through my hair. Instead I pulled up my hood against the wind and hunkered down on the rocks. As a crab scuttled away into a recess, I pictured Miranda, with her fishing net, in pursuit. Yet, had she lived, she'd be beyond that now.

I unscrewed the lid and pulled out the postcard. Held it, a prayer book in my palms, as I stared out to sea. A trawler pricked the horizon and, in the middle distance, seagulls swarmed. I tried to conjure porpoises as I waited for nostalgia to grab me, to swallow me up and spew me out among the waves.

I stared until sea melted into sky, but my soul remained unaltered. I turned my attention to the picture postcard, yet the ranks of beached sun loungers failed to tally with my memories of that holiday. It could've been anywhere.

I flipped the card over. The purple ink was faded along the fold and the neat round letters could have been formed by any earnest child. Even the words, although carefully chosen, were unoriginal. Hardly the essence of her.

I stuffed both card and bottle in my pocket. I'd travelled miles for a reunion with a daughter who'd already gone.

I was hankering after that coffee but it was too soon to turn up at the café. I rose and, slip-sliding on seaweed-strewn rocks, headed for the bank of marram where a zigzag path let me meander through my thoughts. It was daft to concern myself with what Ian thought of me, but I was loath to give him the impression I didn't care. Yet what would he be judging? There's no right way to grieve.

I remembered a quarrel the Christmas after she'd left home. Apart from the terrible twos and teenage door-slamming, it was the only argument we ever had. She berated me for not finding myself a boyfriend after her father had upped sticks. I was flabbergasted: I'd no pretensions to be the perfect mother but I'd never expected to be criticised for putting her needs before mine.

"Don't you see," she snapped, "the burden that puts on me?"

I was too old for romance now, too set in my ways. Ian seemed to tread a similar groove. I'd expected someone older when he mentioned on the phone he was a widower. Someone with wispier hair.

I cast a final glance towards the ocean. The view had scarcely changed: the lonely trawler and the squabbling seabirds. I turned to face the land. Across open pasture, I could make out a low-rise building, with a couple of rustic benches under an awning to the side. I needed that coffee. Ian could think what he liked.

I trudged through the rough grassland. Here and there, among the spikes of coarse grass, I caught a glimpse of pink. Some child, I thought, leaving a trail of sweet wrappers; her mother should have checked her. I looked again: those ruby spots weren't litter but tiny clumps of delicate flowers fighting through the green.

As I neared the café, the flowers thickened to a rosy carpet. Butterflies danced in and out and, up above, a curlew called.

I lowered my hood, let the pale sun stroke my hair. What was the name of that flower? Perhaps Ian would know.

I quickened my pace. Spring had crept up on me unnoticed. Yet, now it had come knocking, how could I not invite it in?

Changed

P. A. Westgate

I was quite nervous when Anna gave me the small recorder. A digital voice recorder she called it. Anna was a nice young woman from City Radio. She had explained that they were asking some local people to keep a sort of diary after the lockdown started and as it changed. The idea was to mark the event with ordinary people's stories. She said she'd write it down and I'd get the chance to read it and she'd change anything I wasn't happy with. She said they were going to get some actors and actresses to read them for the programme. Anna told me just to talk normally whenever I felt like it over the next few months. I wasn't sure. I was quite happy chatting to friends but I said to her that I'd feel a bit silly just talking to myself. Anna said just to imagine I was talking to her. I was quite self-conscious at first but did as Anna had suggested and I soon forgot about the recorder and quite happily chatted away.

When we were told to stay at home we just got on with it. Like most people I suppose. John found he could work just as well at home despite the very flaky internet in these parts. Seemed to prefer it in fact as the weeks went on, converting one of the spare bedrooms into an office. Other than that we really didn't have to make many adjustments to our way of life. We'd never been great ones for going out. Well John wasn't and I just went along with it I suppose. Perhaps the pub of an evening once in a while and sometimes a trip into the city, to the cinema perhaps or, on special occasions, a restaurant. Despite being in the middle of the countryside we rarely walked far from the house. John didn't really want to and I didn't like to by myself. So it wasn't difficult to stop all that. As John said, you couldn't be too careful.

I shop every Friday morning after I'd worked out on the Thursday evening what I'd be cooking for the week ahead. John would drive me to the supermarket and push the trolley around. He seemed quite happy to stay in the car when the supermarket restricted it to one person per trolley. He'd taken to wearing a mask and disposable gloves when we went out and tried to get me to wear them, always telling me to make sure I kept my distance from other shoppers.

I'd never expected John to help with the housework. That was my job while he went out to work. For many years John had done the ironing though. I think he started because he thought he could make a better job of his shirts than I could and he gradually took it all on. It suited me. But I noticed that he began to iron fewer things and after a few weeks of lockdown stopped completely. He didn't need ironed shirts anymore, he told me, as he was only commuting to the converted bedroom and not meeting anyone face-to-face. He said that he didn't see why I needed ironed clothes either as I wasn't going anywhere.

Of an evening we used to sit side-by-side on the settee, sometimes cuddling up, and watch the television but I saw that he preferred one of the armchairs now and left the settee to me. After a couple of months he turned another bedroom into a sort of bed-sitting room and was spending a lot of his time there, when he wasn't in his office. Then he started eating his meals there as well.

I was pleased when the rigid stay-at-home policy was lifted and there was a new set of rules on when and how people could move around. We could start to get back to how we were before all this virus trouble started. I looked forward to meeting people again and going out as we had before and I suppose to John going back to work in the city.

But he didn't go back to work in the city. He said he was getting on quite well at home and anyway the guidance said to work from home if you could. He still took me to the supermarket each week but stayed in the car, even though the one-per-trolley rule had been relaxed, wearing the mask and gloves and with the windows shut. He kept the mask and gloves on when we got home and helped me unload the shopping.

John asked me if I thought he was being unreasonable. Well, I did think he was being just a little silly but over the years I'd found it easier to just let him get on with it when he had a bee in his bonnet.

We've been back to normal more or less for a few weeks now. There are still guidelines around hand washing and facemasks but we only need to keep a metre apart now, which is more or less normal anyway. But John hasn't gone back to normal. He still works at home, saying he prefers it and that he doesn't want to risk the trains and buses. He still spends most of his time upstairs and hardly ever leaves the house. He says he's quite happy up there and doesn't want to go anywhere.

I drive myself to the supermarket these days. I learned to drive when I was still at home but I'd never really driven the car much after I got married. John automatically took the driver's seat when we went out. Now that I've been forced to do it I've found that I like driving and like the freedom it gives me. Now I don't have to do everything in a rush to avoid John's annoyance at being away from home for so long.

I rarely see him these days. It's been a long time since we sat together in front of the telly or went anywhere together. I should feel sad I suppose but I've realised that I don't really care.

I have Rufus now anyway. He's always up for a cuddle on the settee or a walk through our valley or up over the hills into the next. Such walks we have, we're away for hours sometimes. And they like to see him in the pub or when I visit friends. I spend nearly all my time with him now. He's great fun to be with and, you know, I'm doing more things now, going out more than ever I used to and meeting more people. Someone told me that Rufus means red-haired, which I thought very appropriate given that he's covered in rich mahogany-brown hair.

They're recording the programme next week. I told them not bother with an actress to read my piece. I'd do it myself. I'll take Rufus with me, even though he'll have to wait outside. It'll be fun and it's been a while since I've been to the city. We'll go for a long walk when I'm done at the studio and have a look around.

Balcony Views

Margaret Bulleyment

Monday 23 March

"Good morning over there. I'm out here on my balcony. Do come out and say hello. It's quite safe, but don't struggle with the French windows – you have to release the safety catch."

Intrigued by the mystery voice, Iris conquered the windows and stepped out on to her balcony.

"On your left," the voice continued.

She turned to see a smiling, bearded gentleman seated on the next balcony, waving a coffee mug at her. "Adam Hannaford," he bellowed, "on behalf of the Residents' Association – welcome to Myrtle Court."

"Thank you, although I could have timed my arrival better," Iris observed, sitting down with her coffee. "I'm Iris Durrant and dramatic pause – I arrived yesterday in the middle of a coronavirus pandemic."

"Line of the century. You made it just in time, but let's face it, it was worth it. We could be in a much worse place."

"You're right. I've visited a friend here several times and was really impressed. That's partly why I'm here. There's nothing I like better than to be surrounded by gardens and not actually have to be out there anymore, planting and pruning. '*Every apartment has a lounge balcony overlooking the formal courtyard garden and a bedroom view of the more informal gardens and open fields, beyond.*' The brochure was right and whoever designed these apartments knew exactly what they were doing."

"Thank you so much. I designed the whole complex with my son, James. He's the head of the family business now, but I made sure we designed somewhere that I would like to live and I think we got it right."

"You did."

"Now, normally a new resident would be greeted with a full tour – led by me, Chair of the Residents' Association – plus a cocktail, or two, before heading into dinner, but that's all gone to pot for the moment, so I'll have to pass on my pearls of wisdom over coffee. Do you have any questions, or urgent concerns?"

"There's too much to take in at once. Gwen, the manager has explained that we have to stay in our rooms for meals for the moment, but we can go out for a walk round the informal gardens, if we are 'socially distanced'. What a bizarre couple of words those are. Oh, I do have a question. Where's the myrtle bush?"

"What?"

"Myrtle Court must have a myrtle somewhere, or why would it be called that?"

Adam laughed. "Apologies, Iris, but there is no myrtle. It was my mother's name and she loved her garden, so James and I named it after her as we knew she would've loved this place. As it is, we have a Daisy here, a Rose and now an Iris, so our botanical credentials are expanding."

"Rose is my dear friend, but yesterday when I arrived I was told she was not feeling well, so I haven't seen her yet. I'm waiting to find out how she is today. You don't think she's got the virus, do you?"

"Good grief, no. Don't you worry – we're safely cooped up here and looked after beautifully. So long as we don't have to go anywhere near a hospital, we'll all be fine."

"I hope you're right, Adam." She looked down. "It's a beautiful courtyard, but Rose didn't tell me there was a hunky gardener – even if he is old enough to be my grandson."

"That's Guy. Gwen's son. Gwen and Guy. Sounds like a magician's act, doesn't it? Guy was at university, but while he's home here living with his Mum, he's helping in the garden. Gwen's dad owns a garden business and has the contract for supplying plants and maintenance here. We gave this whole project a lot of thought." He paused and waved across the courtyard at another balcony. "Morning, Amy. This is Iris who arrived yesterday."

"Welcome, Iris. I hope you enjoy the show," Amy called.

"Guy gives us a little performance every now and then," said Adam.

"It looks like he's disappeared for the moment," said Iris, "so you may be disappointed."

"We've not been disappointed yet," said Adam. "At least that's what the ladies tell me, and here he comes."

Iris was not sure what she'd expected, but it was certainly not someone in a wet suit, complete with mask, snorkel and flippers, balancing a sound box on his shoulder.

"*In an octopus's garden in the glade*," sang Adam, off key, "or is it shade?" as Guy put the sound box down, stepped into the courtyard pond and started pulling out handfuls of duckweed.

As Guy swung his hips and plunged his arms into the water, residents appeared on their balconies from all sides of the courtyard, laughing and swaying to the music and singing in a whole range of keys.

Iris just laughed and laughed. "Perhaps it should have been Mirth Court."

Adam, gave up on his singing. "A great idea. Do you like music, Iris?"

"Yes. I used to teach it. I brought my electric piano with me, when I saw there wasn't one here."

"The last one died after the Wassail Evening. I look forward to hearing you play when everything's back to normal, but in the meantime this is the best entertainment we can offer."

"Laughing's the best entertainment of all."

"I've an idea," said Adam. "Let's take advantage of this lovely spring weather and meet up again out here this evening, for your welcome cocktail. You can order anything you want with your dinner, you know."

"I've already ordered a cold glass of manzanilla and a bottle of Picpoul for tonight," Iris replied.

"Splendid," said Adam. "We'll get everyone out here. I'll send a message around and then at 6 sharp, we will celebrate your arrival and also celebrate keeping ourselves cheerful. It looks as though we'll not be having any visitors for some time, so it's up to us to keep ourselves amused – with a little help from Guy."

Iris was the first out on her balcony that evening. Below, Guy, now dressed in jeans, was watering a bed of early parrot tulips and whistling to himself. He bowed to Iris over the hosepipe. "Good evening and welcome."

Iris raised her manzanilla to him. "Thank you for the entertainment this morning. I was wondering as I moved in yesterday whether I'd done the right thing in coming here, but after your performance and the temperature of my sherry, I think I might have."

"We aim to please," smiled Guy, disappearing under her balcony.

"Good evening, Iris," announced Adam. "The troops are mustering. We're missing about three people by the looks of it. Cyril… John…"

"One of them will be Rose," said Iris, glancing towards the balcony on her right. "Gwen told me she's still not well. I'm not sure what scared me the most – that news; the fact that Gwen was masked like something out of *Quatermass*; or Boris telling everyone to *Stay Home, Protect the NHS and Save Lives.*"

"Let's forget about that now, but good Boris impression." Adam stood up and waving his glass towards the opposite balconies proclaimed, "Raise your glass to Iris, our newest resident and to our community, which will see off this nasty disruption to our wonderful retirement years. Cheers to the first and bugger off to the second."

As shouts of "Cheers!" and "Bugger off!" bounced around the court, Adam continued. "As it's Mediterranean temperatures, let's all try and eat on our balconies and pretend we're in Spain, Italy…"

"…or the south of France," added Iris. "My Picpoul has just arrived with the dinner. Santé!"

"You're getting into the spirit of this, aren't you," Adam observed. "So where do you hail from, Iris?"

"Born London; lived Sussex, Sweden and Oxfordshire. My husband was a Yorkshireman. My paternal ancestors came from Devon, so here I am." She paused for breath. "I'm guessing you're Devon born and bred, with a name like Hannaford. I have a five times great-grandmother who was a Hannaford.

Hannah, my daughter and her family, just happened to end up in Devon and Rose was one of her neighbours. Rose and I got on so well when I was visiting – we're both music lovers – that when I decided to sell my house and be pampered somewhere, my family and Rose screamed Devon and here I am."

"It's a lovely county. My wife was from Yorkshire too. She never admitted Devon matched up to God's own county of course, but she enjoyed life here." He paused. "Good food, good wine and…" raising his glass, "…good company and we'll get through this.

"As long as the weather holds out, I'm dining on my balcony, Iris. Feel free to join me from your socially distanced one – what a good job we accidentally got that right – for coffee time; lunch time; tea time; dinner time and raise your glasses anytime!"

Hannah? It's Mum. I'm fine. Everyone seems very friendly and in spite of the situation seems determined to keep buggering on and try and have a laugh. No, I haven't spoken to Rose yet, which is worrying. The apartment, the food and the care are top notch – well so they should be at that price.

Thank Rob for all the work he did yesterday heaving the piano and all my stuff up here. I'd never have been able to move in without you both and having done it, I certainly feel more comfortable here with people around me, than I would've been if I was still stuck in Oxfordshire. Give my love to Sophie.

Wednesday 1 April

"Coffee time and Guy's due any minute. Are you coming out, Iris?"

Iris emerged and slumped down at the tiny balcony table. "I've been trying to find out about Rose… and Jill… and John… and Liz… If they're not telling us anything, we have the virus here, don't we?"

"You're probably right, but our friends must be hanging in there, or we would've heard something by now."

"That's no consolation. If Boris in his fifties has it, what chance does Rose aged ninety have?"

"I'm not sure it works that way. Look here's Guy, so let's have a moment of silliness. It is April Fool's Day after all."

As Iris looked down, a crazy red and yellow clown with a fuzzy purple wig stumbled into the courtyard, behind a wheelbarrow that seemed to have a mind of its own. Abandoning the barrow beside the pergola, he ran round the path, leapt over a seat, climbed the rockery and losing his balance, narrowly missed falling into the pond.

"What's that music? I know it, I know it." said Adam.

"*Entry of the Gladiators*. Circus music."

The music died away as Guy moved back to the pergola, his head drooping and then as the sound box began serenading the garden with *Don't Laugh at Me 'Cause I'm a Fool*, quietly sang along.

"Norman Wisdom," enthused Adam. "I loved him when I was a kid. I spent hours trying to walk like him."

Iris looked around and sighed. "There are fewer people out here today. You know what that means."

"Well, yes, but we need to stay calm and positive… oh look…"

Guy the clown stopped singing, opened the sack in his wheelbarrow and released a cloud of multi-coloured balloons.

"We need to know if they have the virus," Iris insisted. "What we don't need," she shouted, as a red balloon drifted past her balcony, "are people trying to distract us by treating us like children."

Hannah? No, I'm not all right. I can't find anything out about Rose. I'm sure she has Covid-19 and I'm sure others have it too. But no one is saying anything and they're trying to distract us with 'fun' things. Worst of all, I got really mad at my neighbour, Adam, who was trying to cheer me up. After a week eating, drinking, chatting four times a day out on our balconies and walking round the gardens identifying plants with him at a distance, I suddenly turn on him. I've spent all day sulking in my room like a moody teenager. I'm so ashamed of myself.

Thursday 2 April

Hannah? Yes, I am in a state. I've had the most awful day. I went out on the balcony for coffee time this morning and to apologise to

Adam for yesterday, but he didn't appear. He didn't appear at lunch time either, so now I'm really worried that he's ill. I've been playing Bach all afternoon, but even Bach has his limits when you're worried about your friends. Sophie wants to talk to me? That would be lovely.

Sophie? How's my Picklepuss? I'm so sorry we can't have a proper hug. Granny's been practising her piano this afternoon. I hope you're practising too and then we can play duets when all this chaos is over.

Friday 3 April

Iris leaned over her balcony and peered around the courtyard. There were fewer people out there yet again. Adam had not appeared at coffee time and there was still no sign of him. She would eat her lunch inside and have another afternoon playing the piano.

"Iris? Don't go back in, I'm just coming out. I'd forgotten my wine."

"Adam, you're okay?"

"Of course, I'm okay. Something disagreed with me yesterday, but I'm fine today and I really enjoyed the music."

"I'm so sorry. I assumed you'd succumbed to the virus, been carted off to the medical wing and that I had two empty rooms either side. If I'd known you were there, I would've used my headphones."

"Don't worry. In fact, throw your headphones away whenever you want to play and let's hear it."

"Adam, please listen. I must apologise for my stupid behaviour on Friday. I was really upset yesterday when you didn't appear and I'd left you on such an unpleasant note."

"Yesterday's pleasant notes more than made up for it, so please don't worry, Iris. You're always worrying. Now let's raise our glasses to the others and enjoy our lunch. However silly the world is, we can outdo it."

Thursday 9 April

Hello? Hannah? Thank you, my love. It's the strangest birthday I've ever had, but at least it will be a memorable one. Parcels arriving this morning? How exciting. No, I don't mind just talking. Don't worry. I know if we'd had time, Rob would have set up Skype for me, but we were lucky that I even got moved in, so I really don't mind. I can talk to you at least and you know what I'm like with computers. I would've messed it up from the beginning. It's not like I don't know what you look like. Sophie's going to play me some Mozart? That's wonderful. I'm listening.

"Morning, Iris. Where are you?"

"I'm coming. I was on the phone with the family listening to my granddaughter playing the piano."

"Happy Birthday!"

"How did you know?"

"Aah. Well, Rose told me you'd a special birthday coming up and she was planning something for you. Everything might have completely changed, but we can still celebrate in our funny little way. There'll be champagne tonight, but in the meantime da-didda-dum-dum-DUM – there's Guy!"

With Bizet bursting his way out of the sound box, there was Guy, resplendent in very tight trousers, a glittery top and a battered black hat with ear muffs attached, waving a red scarf at the wheelbarrow which had sprouted horned handles. As Guy pranced and strutted, a rose in his teeth, the balcony residents gave their all to the toreador's chorus, waving red skirts, towels and even a feather boa.

Iris rushed inside grabbed her red dressing gown and joined in. As the music reached its climax, Guy bowed very low in front of Iris's balcony and a different sound pulsed around the courtyard as a drone dropped out of the sky and neatly deposited a box of red roses at Iris's feet.

Iris was speechless as she unwrapped the bouquet – complete with mini hand sanitiser – and read a card signed by Adam. *Roses are red, irises blue, I couldn't get irises, hope these will do. (I'm colour blind anyway.)*

As the residents warbled *Happy Birthday*, Iris sat down bemused.

"Thank you so much, Adam, how on earth did you…?"

"When the university's Drone Club President is your gardener, anything is possible."

"You're incorrigible."

"I aim to please."

"I just wish…"

"…that Rose was here. I know. She's a lovely lady."

"Do you know her well? Has she told you her story? Her childhood?"

"I seem to remember her telling me she was born in Singapore? China?"

"China. Her parents were missionaries. Her father would go round preaching in villages and Rose could remember seeing women hobbling painfully along on bound feet and children with bellies swollen from hunger. She saw dangerous times too when the Red Army were marching through. Her parents sent her to boarding school in Shanxi when she was seven and left here there. They never visited, or contacted her once.

"Three months before Pearl Harbor, a teacher told her that her father had died. When the Japanese arrived, the headmaster was arrested and thrown in prison; the army took over the school buildings and the pupils were sent to an internment camp, which housed two thousand adults and children. In her first week, she saw a man electrocuted while trying to escape over the perimeter barbed wire.

"She was in the camp for nearly four years. She worked in the laundry, scrubbing and hanging out the washing, which froze in the winter. Winters were very cold and summers unbearably hot. Food was short and they would swallow teaspoons of ground egg shells for calcium.

"In 1945, when the camp was liberated, she ended up on a hospital ship in Hong Kong harbour with osteomyelitis and became a guinea pig for penicillin to treat it.

"When the internees' ship docked in Liverpool, Rose didn't recognise the mother who came to meet her. That same mother refused to talk about her daughter's internment years and told her she was ashamed of her, when Rose said she would have nothing to do with the religion that had ruined her life.

"She suffered from low self-esteem for years and years and was in her fifties before she sought counselling. After that came some sort of acceptance and she wrote a book about her childhood when she realised it was a forgotten chapter of the war. She said that writing it gave her peace for the first time. I've a copy if you'd like to read it."

"What can I say after all that? I'd love to read it. Who would have thought that Rose had gone through all that?"

Sunday 12 April Easter Day

Hannah? No, it's not Happy Easter. Our dear friend Rose has died. I can't talk now. Sophie's Easter egg is in the cupboard under your stairs. Give her my love.

"Iris? Please come out, I need to talk to you."

"I'm only coming out for a moment. I'm not up to Guy dressed as a rabbit, or whatever's happening today."

"Nothing's happening today. We've all heard the sad news about Rose and today is cancelled."

"Adam, we all abandoned Rose – like everyone else in her life. After her appalling childhood she deserved happiness. When she married and had two children, that was as normal as her life ever got, until her husband left her and her children both moved to the other side of the world. She was alone nearly all her life and then she died alone and I'm just devastated. I can't talk any more now."

Sunday 3 May

"Morning, Iris, would you believe there's almost good news in the paper today?"

"I've already seen it. Capt. Tom, veteran soldier, has raised £32 million for the NHS since walking round his garden for his 100th birthday and the Prime Minister admits he nearly died."

"I was thinking more that tests are on their way; deaths are dropping day by day and the drug that treats ebola might be good for corona. There's also the fact that hard as it is, we've only had four deaths here and we're not suffering shortages of masks and protective gear, so whatever we say, it could be a lot worse."

"That's what you always say but…"

"Let it go, Iris, it won't bring Rose, George, Tom, or Cyril back, we have to move on."

"I'm know you're right, but I can't do it."

"You can. Let's enjoy whatever Guy has cooked up for us today. There are more of us out here again."

"You're so positive, Adam, I could strangle you."

"I thought you said that was what my singing sounded like. Here comes Guy. Release your inner child. Oh, hang on, he's just wearing jeans and a top and carrying a fork, so nothing might be happening after all."

Guy put down his fork, switched on his sound box wiggled his hips and slowly began taking off his sweater.

"I know that. It's *The Stripper.* Surely not? Da-da-daa-da-da-da-daa…"

"No way Adam, he's still got his jeans on. No, no, he's down to his pants and what's that banner he's waving, you've got better eyesight?"

"International Naked Gardening Day 2020 – I love it."

"Why is he wrapping it around… oh he's taken his pants off and I think Amy may be about to throw herself over her balcony," screamed Iris.

The courtyard erupted in cheers, laughter and clapping as Guy waved his pants, grabbed his sound box and disappeared backwards out of the courtyard.

Iris was still laughing. "Okay you win, I laughed a lot."

"Well done, I knew you could do it."

Tuesday 2 June

"You're still struggling, aren't you Iris?"

"Yes I am, because all this talk of tests to see if you've had it, is scaring me."

"Why?"

"Think about it. Rose was the first to contract the virus. There were no people discharged from hospital here and no staff member had it until the end of March. She fell ill five days after I visited her."

"You mean you think you gave it to her?"

"Yes, I think I killed her."

"Iris for goodness sake, that's totally ridiculous, it could've come from anywhere – a contaminated letter, or something. Even if it came from someone outside, why on earth would it be you?"

"Because I've done the same thing before."

"You've lost me, completely."

"Killed someone. When I was about eight, I wanted a brother, or sister, but my mother said that was not possible, she couldn't have any more children, although she would like to. When I was a teenager, I answered the door one day to a friend of Mum's who wanted to talk to her. Mum was upstairs and when I found her she was sorting files in the bedroom – there were piles of paper everywhere. Mum went down to see her friend and as I was leaving the room, I tripped over one of the piles. On top was a consultation report from the hospital where I was born. It turns out I would've been a twin, but something happened and my twin was 'absorbed' by me. I know that sounds crazy, but it's called a vanishing twin. It usually happens early in the pregnancy, but in Mum's case it was later.

"Perhaps if my parents had told me when I was old enough to understand, it would have been different; but they never told me and I never told them I knew. It was forty years later when both my parents were dead, before I told anyone. Hannah was the first to know. All these years I've had this guilt that I killed my twin. How could we both have grown in the same womb for me to become the stronger one and to take over what should have been her life?

"Rose was the second person I told. I think one of the reasons we bonded was that we both had a shadow over our childhoods. I thought, like Rose, that I'd buried that shadow by telling her and Hannah about it, but this pandemic nightmare has brought it back to the surface."

"Oh, Iris. What can I tell you? What are the death figures now? 40,000? Every one of those people was infected by something, or someone and infected other people themselves – that's a lot of guilt – but we'll never know. There's going to be more people infected and even more people who will die because important medical consultations were cancelled. Then they'll be enquiries into why the government didn't do this, or that, differently and what we can learn from it and it'll go on for years and years, long after we have popped our clogs. And some lessons will be learned and some things will be forgotten – until the next time it happens. You and Rose enjoyed your friendship and that's all that matters. There's nothing more you can do, except not feel guilty. You owe it to her."

"I want to believe you."

"Why spoil the rest of your life wrestling with things you cannot do anything about? Unless we live in the moment, we're wasting precious time. Come on, when you arrived you were so positive. Anyway, it's time for today's entertainment. It took a bit of organising, but I think you're going to like it. Make sure you've got your Picpoul handy."

"There's certainly a lot of residents gathering on their balconies, this morning."

"Here comes Guy and his barrow."

"Why on earth is he wearing a dress, red shoes and has a stuffed dog tied to his head?"

"Because he needs his arms for other things. Listen."

"*Somewhere over the Rainbow*, I get it. My song."

Guy stood beside the pond, waving his arms until he was satisfied that all the residents were singing enthusiastically and then he unfurled a great rainbow banner and stood aside as a couple and a teenager with linked arms appeared beside the rockery and moving to the music, slowly wound their way across the courtyard.

"That's my James, his wife Fiona and grandson, Mark." Adam waved and blew kisses down to them. "You can see Mark gets his impeccable sense of rhythm from me. Keep your eyes peeled, Iris. It's your turn next."

"But that's Hannah, Rob and my dear Sophie. What a wonderful surprise!" Iris leaned as far out as she dared, as her family swayed below. "You can see my Sophie has dancing lessons, can't you?" she laughed.

Family followed family and finally Amy's family arrived with a trio of flute, clarinet and side drum. Playing in an entirely different key from Guy's sound box, it brought the whole procession to a glorious cacophonous climax.

Guy left his banner wrapped around the pond wall and with his customary flourish bowed low in each direction to the residents, before tottering out of sight in his red shoes.

Adam stood up and raising his glass in three directions shouted, "After just one day with us, my friend Iris here, nicknamed us Mirth Court. I suggest we adopt that name permanently. What do we say, now, Mirth Court?"

"Cheers and bugger off!" chorused the residents in unison, waving their glasses.

Iris rose to her feet. "Thank you, Adam," she proclaimed, "for keeping us positive – the only kind of positive we want to be."

"Thank you, Adam and cheers!" came the reply.

"What did you mean by your song, Iris?" enquired Adam, as the courtyard quietened down.

"Well, I hate to tell you as you've had me florally connected for the past three months, but my name, Iris, is nothing to do with the flower – it's a Greek 'rainbow'.

"Ah, interesting. I've no idea what Adam means, but you're going to tell me aren't you?"

"I certainly am. It's Hebrew for red earth, or just – man."

"In that case, with my serious lack of botanical knowledge, I'd better settle for just man."

Ghost Training

Anne Wilson

I got the best job in the world, the one I always wanted. Bodger liked the Waltzer and Noddy always worked on the Dodgems but for me and Raffe the Ghost Train was the only ride.

Mad Murphy ran the Ghost Train, twelve cars; four going through, four outside and four spare, he always said. He showed us how to hide inside in the dark, and give the customers more thrills for their money, from the first scream and the laughing when the doors opened, to the rattling and banging as the cars came back out. Those noises were automatic but we learnt how to touch people's arms or their hair very lightly, and make noises of our own from behind the open coffin lid. Two shillings and sixpence was a lot for people to pay. Getting the timing right as the cars came through was very important. We draped sheets over ourselves and moaned beside the headstones. 'Ghost training', Mad Murphy called it; his little joke.

Raffe and me did Friday nights, Saturdays and Sundays, and weekdays as well when we dared. Snoopy Snodgrass, the Truant Man, was always after us, knocking on our doors, but we were too quick for him. Even our mums were out. They all worked except Noddy's. She was at home with his two brothers and two sisters and she was going to have another one but then she wasn't. She liked Noddy to be off school because he could go to the Co-op and get stuff for his little brothers and sisters and Woodbines. Sometimes he opened the pack and took one out and she pretended she hadn't noticed. The time when she didn't have the baby there was a lot going on at Noddy's house and my mum let him stay for a few days, then he went home.

Bodger's mum worked on the whelk stall and we used to have as many cockles and winkles as we could eat. I think they'd been drowned in the vinegar. Raffe's mum worked in Fred's Fresh Fish Bar so we got chips as well, red hot, in newspaper that made your hands all black. I wished my mum could have worked on the candy floss but she got a job in Woolworths in the High Street, on the Max Factor. She said it was a really good job.

"Mikey," she used to say, "I know one day you'll get an even better job than mine."

She gave me money to buy ice-cream soda or Coca cola after school but I used to save it for smokes and ask Raffe's mum for a drink.

Our old teacher, Mr Smailes, Smelly Smalls we called him, used to give us extra homework but we never did it. He said we'd never get jobs; I wish he could see me now. I'm good at what I do. I can make the lights flicker and go out and when the car goes through darkness. I've got a special hissing noise I make in the back of my throat. If I'm riding the car I can lean over and touch the girl's knees, and thighs as well if their dress is really short. They always blame their boyfriends for that but then they hold them tighter and make little screaming noises.

Jacqueline Sowerby used to scream a lot. She used to squeeze your arm till it hurt. One day she squeezed my leg and I wanted to go round again and again. Her sister, Louise, let me kiss her, but I liked Jacqueline the best. She had really long hair and you could reach under it and touch her breast and pretend it was an accident.

Girls aren't so easily frightened these days but I catch at their hair and touch their bare arms and necks. Sometimes I get so excited and laugh so hard, I shake about and make a shrieking noise. People used to say it was called 'being hysterical'.

That last summer that we were all together, Bodger, Noddy, Raffe and me, was the summer that Louise Sowerby said she was pregnant. She said it was either mine or Bodger's but Bodger said they never did it but he's a liar. Louise said it was most likely mine because she liked me the best so I said "maybe" but I didn't think we'd done it right. Louise kept asking for a cigarette and I kept explaining that you have that after, but she kept asking. We were under the pier and she got sand in her hair. She said my hair was like Billy Fury's and it was a pity I couldn't sing. We'd been to see Saturday Night and Sunday Morning at the Gaumont picture house but I couldn't remember it afterwards because we sat on the back row and we were just necking all through the film. Louise kept holding my hands but I managed to get one under her skirt and she let me touch her knickers. Jacqueline wouldn't go to the pictures with me, then she started seeing someone older from the Grammar School who was starting work in an office.

We didn't earn a lot on the fairground but the girls used to gather round on Friday and Saturday nights and we'd give them free rides. We usually ended the night on the dodgems where Noddy worked. That's why we called him Noddy, because the cars were little fat red and yellow ones. The music there was the loudest and the sparks from the grid above fizzed and crackled like fireworks on Bonfire Night. Louise wouldn't go on the dodgems after she said she was pregnant; she just sat on the rails and smoked. She wouldn't go on the Waltzer either. That was Bodger's ride and he was the most popular with the girls. I think she didn't like to see him flirting and getting chatted up. I think she was jealous.

I don't know where the others are now. I sometimes think I see Bodger when the cars on the Waltzer are spinning round really fast making everything look blurred. He used to ride with them and spin them faster and faster, going up and down and round and round. I remember his favourite shirt and I think I can see the colours flying by, but then I can't. I've never seen Noddy on the dodgems but I'm sure I've heard his laugh late at night when the sparks are flying. He had a really funny laugh that made everyone else laugh as well.

Once, Raffe came and tried to help me on the Ghost Train. He hid inside the coffin but I wouldn't allow that; the job's just mine now. I made a sort of growling noise, a new one I've learnt how to do and I do it when I get mad. I get mad more and more, I don't know why. Anyway, he got the message all right. He won't be coming back. He said I'd changed a lot and he didn't hardly know me. He said everything had changed. He looked lost and he said he was going to look for Bodger. I don't know if he found him. I felt a bit sorry after.

I used to get mad mostly in school when old Smelly Smalls tried to get me to read. The letters used to get mixed up all the time and I wondered if my book was different to everyone else's. The others laughed at me so I sometimes didn't go to the class even when I was in school. I used to sit in the toilets but they were even smellier than old Smelly's classroom.

My Dad was a stevedore on the docks; went to work on the tram. He said he never did any reading and writing and he was bringing home a decent wage, so I didn't feel so bad, except my sister was three years younger than me and she was always reading stupid girls' books. She kept them all in a row on her bedroom shelf just to show off; she wasn't allowed on the fairground. I got some railway track and an engine and a carriage one Christmas. I made a tunnel and painted skulls and daggers inside it to frighten the passengers.

All I wanted to do was work on the Ghost Train, riding the cars and hearing the music and making the noises. I couldn't read or write well but I could count money. When he went for a drink, Mad Murphy used to leave me in charge of the kiosk. I always hoped Jacqueline Sowerby would see me in the kiosk but I don't think she ever did. If she had, she might have gone out with me.

The things that make me mad now are couples necking all the time in the cars instead of being scared by my special effects. Girls that look like Jacqueline Sowerby make me mad. Other boys touching them make me mad. I get really upset when some people don't scream at all. If they just laugh, I want to kill them.

The man who replaced Mad Murphy doesn't pay me, or the one after him, or the one after him, though I'm getting better and better and stronger and stronger, but I don't need money. My Dad was right about not needing to read as well; except I would have liked to read what they wrote in the *Gazette*, those men who came to take photos after everything happened. I tried to make sure I was in some of the photos by standing as close as I could to what they were photographing. I stood next to Louise and her stomach was really big. She cried a lot. That black stuff girls put on their eyes was all over her face. I don't know if she had the baby okay. I didn't see her or Jacqueline again after that. I think the others were there, Bodger, Noddy and Raffe, it's hard to remember.

I can't remember whose idea it was to go on the Big Dipper that day. I'd never been on it before. People went on for a dare. It was supposed to be the highest in the country. We didn't usually spend our money on the rides, just worked our own.

We were calling ourselves a gang that summer. We were all celebrating because we'd left school for ever. There was another gang, worked in the animal house in Blackpool Tower. They'd started coming to the fairground and hanging round the rides. They didn't speak proper English. We all got on the Dipper but me and Bodger and Noddy and Raffe managed to get the best car. There was always a scramble for the last one.

As we went over the top our car dropped back down again. I thought it was part of the ride because my eyes were closed, because it was hard to breathe, but I heard Bodger shouting and Noddy started screaming. I'd never heard him scream before. I've been practising his scream and I think I sound just like him. I think Raffe managed to stand up then fell out of the car. It all happened so fast. Then I think we must have come off the rails. Everything was broken, us and the car. I could see bits of us lying on the tracks and underneath the scaffolding. I remember thinking, funny how it didn't hurt. I wanted to look good in the photos because I'd never been photographed before except at school.

That last summer together seems a long time ago, and then sometimes it doesn't. People dress different now. They're not the same. They don't scream as much but I'm getting some new ideas how to make them. I'm working on showing myself the way I was the last time I saw myself, underneath the scaffolding. I think that would make them scream.

Homeland

Anne Wilson

Published by FTB Press, Irrational Fears, August 2015

"What is it Kim?"

Pete looks concerned, but I don't want to talk about it; I don't ever want to talk about it; not now, not ever.

I twitch again, only slightly but visibly and my hand goes to my stomach. It feels as if I have been poked by something or accidentally knocked. The strange, unwelcome sensation makes my heart beat faster and bile rises in my throat. I swallow it back, feeling a little choked and panicky. I smell antiseptic.

"Don't worry," I say. "It's okay, it never lasts very long." But the truth is, I actually think it may be getting worse.

I did visit the doctor when the feelings began. At first, they kept me awake at night. The doctor decided it was caused by indigestion and gave me a prescription for tablets for antacid relief. When that didn't work, I went back, and he gave me some tablets to calm my nerves and help me sleep better. They didn't work either, so he gave me a stronger prescription. I think he thought I was attention seeking.

Later, sitting on the metro on the way home, I had time to think and the realisation that I was on my own with this situation and always would be crystalized slowly. I had read in a magazine about someone who had a phantom pregnancy and thought maybe what I had was something similar. Hers was all inside her head which is where mine must be too.

I decided I'd like to try a holiday, a change of air, a change of scene, maybe a change of diet. Pete and I deserved some quality time together. Well he did anyway; he'd been working such long hours away from home. I booked us a cheap week in Spain. It even occurred to me that a solution to my problem might be to try and get pregnant and a holiday could be romantic. Pete would be pleased. He would take such good care of me. I bought a new dress and some sun preparations.

I change my position on the beach towel, but my heart feels twisted, my stomach trembles and the paella I have just eaten seems to shift uncomfortably, feels as if it's liquefying somewhere inside me. I sit up and move my hand involuntarily from my stomach to my chest.

Pete becomes more concerned; slips a comforting arm around my shoulders. "Have you been taking those tablets the doctor gave you; the stronger ones? You did bring them, didn't you?"

"Yes," I answer miserably, but it's a lie. I brought them, but they aren't working either. They're in the bin in the hotel bathroom. I'll make sure they're covered up when we get back.

A young family from our hotel are a little further along the beach. Their baby cries out suddenly and I jump involuntarily. Pete laughs, but not unkindly. Pete would do anything for me and the simple knowledge of that adds to my unhappiness. I don't deserve him. More to the point, he doesn't deserve me.

"As soon as we get home, I'm coming to the doctor's with you. You haven't been yourself since I came back from training." He smooths out our towels and offers me a bottle of water.

I shake my head and lie back down; try to relax. How could I ever have deceived him the way I did?

When I found out that my one drunken night with his best friend while Pete was away on an army training course had made me pregnant, I was absolutely horrified. How did things like this happen? By the time Pete returned, my dates would be all wrong. It couldn't be explained. I couldn't allow this situation to continue. I couldn't tell my friends or ask my parents for help and with every day that passed I panicked more and more.

I found the telephone number of the clinic. They fitted in an appointment just two days later. I went on my own for the consultation and returned the following week for the termination. I wasn't sure what to take with me and felt terrified. Everything smelled of antiseptic, even the flowers in the vase on the table in the waiting room. I remember trying to wipe the streaks of mascara from under my eyes and a nurse giving me a box of tissues. I remember my hands trembling.

Afterwards I cried and cried. I felt hollow, as if they'd taken away too much of my insides. I'd never felt more alone. I didn't expect to care so much; after all, if this pregnancy had continued it would have ruined my life and yet now it was over, I felt more alone than I'd ever felt. Alone and haunted by my thoughts.

Pete returned, and our lives carried on as normal. His friend didn't know what had happened or what I'd been through and on the rare occasions we met he gave no sign of even remembering our drunken fling. He never gave me any reason to worry that he might tell Pete the truth.

"Shall we go back to the hotel and get ready for dinner? Don't want you to overdo the sunbathing; especially if you're feeling a bit fragile." Pete still looks worried.

"I'm okay now," I lie.

I sit up and begin to gather my things together. "I think I had hiccups. You remember saying the paella had a funny taste at lunchtime? You were probably right. Let's go out to a restaurant tonight and have a change."

"Good idea," Pete says, shaking our sandy beach towels and folding them up. "You go in the bathroom first and have a long soak. You haven't worn your new dress yet; how about wearing it tonight?"

I smile and nod my head. The weird feeling has left me for now and each time it goes, I hope desperately that it won't return. I never really thought it was caused by indigestion, but I suppose it could be nerves. If only I could relax and move on from what happened, I wouldn't need to see the doctor again, wouldn't need sleeping tablets.

I retrieve my half empty little bottle of tranquillizers out of the bathroom bin and resolve to take them again. I need all the help I can get. I take a double dose to start me off. Don't want any more dreams about phantom pregnancies.

The unfamiliar bathroom has wall to floor tiling with a sort of grey marble vein running through it. Not what I would have chosen, but I suppose it looks all right here. I wonder if all the bathrooms are exactly the same. Four hundred and seventy bathrooms, with four towels in each one; two bath size; two hand size and a towelling bath-mat. That must mean… how many towels…

I suppose I drift off out of things a bit. The tranquillizers, and the atmosphere in here is all steamy because I shut the door and the air extraction vent doesn't seem to work, just rattles a lot.

I left Pete lying on the bed in his underpants, watching a football match. Someone scores a goal, I can hear the crowd's elation and the mattress on the bed protesting as Pete bounces up and down. After a while he shouts to ask if I'm all-right.

"Fine! Thanks!" I open my eyes and sit further up the bath. The feeling has come back, stronger than ever. My whole body stiffens as I feel the sensation of my belly being softly nudged, very gently prodded.

I look down, expecting marks to be showing on my skin and imagine I see them, tiny and pale. I look at the toilet bowl beside the bath and wonder if I might be sick. The smell of antiseptic is strong in here. Must be to cover up the drains.

Then I become aware of an amorphous thing, floating in the steam above my body. The edges are translucent, but slowly I see a curving core, rubbery jelly, like a grub with a large head.

My feet and legs go rigid as I try to push myself backwards up the bath, away from it. I crack my elbow against the damp tiled wall and can't supress a sharp yelp of pain just as another goal is scored. I can hear my heartbeat and feel pressure in my chest from holding in the scream which would bring Pete hammering on the bathroom door. I look around me wildly, fighting panic and nausea.

The thing drops downwards and bumps itself against my naked wet belly.

I am trapped in the bath with a scream trapped in my throat.

The thing nudges against me again like a glutinous, misshapen soap bubble. I can see it has two black dots for eyes and buds where the limbs would have formed; it's on the outside trying to get back in, back home.

The Rise of the Zenoton

Gill James

Torbis watched the older Zenton as he looked again at the figures. The snake-like curls on Karlik's head twisted and turned pink, a sure sign that he was worried about what he saw.

"It's that bad, sir?" said Torbis.

Karlik nodded, his locks now fiery red. Torbis had only ever seen that happen once before on his own father when their home had been burnt to the ground by the rebel mob who had invaded the Holik quarter where he and his family lived back then. At least there were no rebels now that a good health-care system had been introduced and the worry that droids would take over the menial work and leave people unemployed had shown itself to be unfounded; they'd found other things for the newly unemployed Zenoton to do. On the whole much pleasanter things than emptying rubbish, mining salt or working in factories.

Fortunately nobody in Torbis's family had been hurt. They'd managed to build another fine home but his father had never quite got over losing the first one. His curls had never glowed golden again.

Karlik's locks continued to redden. "It's worse than we expected. We've never had anything like this on Zenoto before. It's deadlier even than the Covid-19 disease on Terrestra in 2020, worse even than the Peace Child disease they had after the poison cloud lifted. It kills and it kills quickly and painfully. The death rate is doubling every two days and newer cases are tripling every day."

"Which means the death rate will rise even higher?"

Karlik nodded.

"What can we do sir?"

"Isolate. Introduce social distancing."

"Can't we find a cure? Or a vaccine?"

"Well of course our scientists are working on that but it may take some time."

Torbis nodded. "What do you mean by isolating? And social distancing?"

"Everyone must stay at home. People should only go out to shop, for medical reasons and for a little exercise each day. Droids will man the shops, do deliveries, deal with the dead and manage the nursing." Karlik's locks had faded now to a gentler pink.

"Will people do that?"

"They'll have to or they'll be punished. It worked on Terrestra twice." One lock went bright red again. He sighed. "At least we have droids. The Terrestrans had hardly any in 2020 and they didn't have enough in 3025."

"But if people can't go out, they can't go to work and they can't earn money."

Karlik nodded. "That is something we have to bring up in the Council tomorrow."

"Furlough," said Karlik. "We must furlough those people who can't work from home."

Torbis held his breath as he watched the assembled council of the twenty Zenoton primary executives. They were all frowning and one or two of them were showing pink locks.

"How will that work? Where will we get the money from?" The Zenoton treasurer looked surprisingly calm and his locks remained a neutral purple.

"The banks."

"Will they have enough?"

"If not we must borrow from other planets."

There was a lot of mumbling. Now the treasurer's locks glowed red. "The planetary debt will be enormous."

"So be it. Better to have a planet full of life and huge debt than no debt and no life."

It was agreed in the end: every person on the planet would receive enough money to live on. The droids would do all of the necessary work to maintain Zenoton life. Zenotons would enjoy a period of enforced leisure. Until they had this virus under control and the deaths and new cases ceased or until they had a cure and /

or a vaccine. The scientists would of course carry on working and they would be richly rewarded with a period of extended leisure after it was all over.

"There will be quite a few problems at first, I'd imagine." Karlik went to touch Torbis's shoulder then pulled his arm away. "I'm afraid we politicians will have to continue to work. Remotely of course. I expect we're going to get inundated with problems."

On cue, Torbis received a message that a video call was waiting for him.

Kalrik nodded. "Here we go."

Torbis recognised at once the reporter from the Holik Observer. Ah, so journalists were still at work. Naturally. Her locks were glowing pink. "I'd really like to speak to Executive Karlik."

"He's rather tied up for the day, I'm afraid. I can speak on his behalf."

"All right." Her locks danced in a frenzy but at least they didn't go red. "I'm getting a lot of reports that the banks aren't offering some younger people the grants the Council promised."

"Oh?"

"Yes, they're saying there's no security on them."

This was annoying. The instruction had been that anybody who applied for the cost of living grant should be given it. No questions asked. And there was no need for any sort of security. Everyone was entitled to it.

"I'll look into it straight away."

"You'd better. Or you'll have some deaths on your conscience. And I don't mean from the virus." She disappeared from the screen.

That was one bitter young reporter.

"Contact Central Bank," Torbis commanded.

Is a split second he was face to face with the chief executive of the largest bank on Zenoto. The power that his post in Karlik's office brought him still amazed him.

The chief executive nodded in agreement when he explained the problem. "I know. But our hands are tied. We have to do something to stop all of our money bleeding away."

“You mean you’re deliberately finding reasons not to award the grants the Council has sanctioned?”

The older Zenoton nodded. “We just don’t have enough money to offer everything you’ve promised.”

“Well, have you applied to other planets for loans?”

“Of course. It’s the first thing we did. But it takes time. And there’s no guarantee we’ll get them.”

“You’ve got to keep trying and you must chase them up.”

“Naturally.”

The man’s head turned pink and his locks were squirming. Well that wasn’t surprising. He should let him get on. “Will you report to me again tomorrow?”

The other Zenoton bowed slightly. “With pleasure.”

Torbis ended the call.

“I see what you mean,” said Karlik. Torbis had spent the last twenty minutes telling him about the conversation with the bank’s executive and the problem he’d highlighted. “But what can we do? I’m reluctant to create artificial credits.”

It was so obvious to Torbis. He didn’t know why his boss couldn’t see it straight away. “We should suspend money.”

“Suspend money? What do you mean?”

“Well, for example, a family would no longer need to pay their rent. Their landlord wouldn’t have to pay any service charge. If there’s a leak the plumber comes and fixes it for no payment and he doesn’t have to worry because he doesn’t have to pay for parts, he doesn’t have to pay his rent either and he doesn’t have to pay for what he picks up at the supermarket. In fact, if no one had to pay at the supermarkets it might even keep the queues down and help us to further keep this virus under control.”

Karlik nodded. “Though I’m not sure we can go quite that far. Certainly, though, we’ll stop people paying rents and stop all the payments that the landlords have to make. See how that goes.”

There were 70,000 landlords on the video link. They had created a communication override so that they were all forced to join in. That also meant that actually the only ones who weren't there were the ones who were dying from the effects of the virus. He was glad his droid assistant had muted all of the mics. He was glad too that he couldn't see them though it was eerie to think that they could all see him. The only time he'd been in such a big video conference before was when the Council had gone live. There were then of course multiple executives and aides also present. He'd never had to chair his own meeting before.

After he'd given a little explanation about how this would all work the questions poured in. The dataserve aligned them and he was able to make comments on what was perceived to be the more pressing concerns.

What will happen to my mortgage payments?

"They are suspended from now until the crisis is over. But payments will be credited to your account just as if you'd made them."

What if I have to have a deep clean because someone has had the virus?

"Tradesmen are included in the scheme. You will still use your expertise as a landlord to find the right skilled worker for the task to ensure work is done to a correct standard. But there will be no financial outlay."

What about if my tenant is a nuisance in some way. Can I ask them to leave?

That was a tricky one. It was certainly true that nuisance tenants were usually the same ones who didn't pay rent. And if they didn't pay rent the landlords had the ultimate excuse for getting rid of them. "We don't want to make people homeless, especially at this time of crisis. But we will help you to re-educate your tenants." Torbis dreamed of a time when there would be no more antisocial behaviour on Zenoto.

Time ran out but he did manage to answer over fifty questions.

"Shall I enable mics and cameras so that you can judge the mood?" his droid operative asked.

"Yes please."

At once he saw a sea of faces that looked reasonably happy.

Locks were glowing mainly green and blue. They were quite calm, then. "Your mics have been enabled. Let me know what you think." Most people started clapping. They began to leave the meeting one by one. He waited until the last one had gone before he left himself.

He ought now to cancel the payment for his own rent. He hesitated for a moment. What about if he went on paying it? His credits weren't under threat. But no, that would be silly. It would just be a computer exercise. He signed himself into his bank account and stopped his regular payment for his rent.

Everything seemed to be working smoothly at the supermarket. There was no panic. Droids gently enforced the two metre rule in the queue outside. There were no queues at the checkouts but customers did have to walk in front of a Zenoton guard who stopped every tenth shopper and inspected what they had in their unit. Torbis was there today to see how that was going. He felt a little uncomfortable in his personal protective suit. It stopped him moving easily. He felt sorry for the guard who had to wear this for up to eight universal hours a day.

He smiled to himself. This all showed that he had been right all along; suspend money for one sector and you had to do if for everyone. The plumber who fixed the leak couldn't pay his suppliers who couldn't pay their children's school fees. The school then couldn't pay the teachers, who couldn't pay the plumber to fix the leak. In the end, leaks must be fixed, children must be educated and teachers needed to eat.

"Why don't they all get their groceries delivered?" he asked the guard.

The guard shrugged. "I guess they like to get out and to make personal choices. Even though there's a risk."

He watched the loaded baskets and trolleys going past. They all seemed to have only the finest produce.

"How does that work?" he asked the guard. "Are people being greedy?"

"Well, no. We're here to stop that. But they're only producing the best quality now. Why should anyone put up with less than the best?"

"But how can we keep up production?"

"More and more droids. They soon won't need people like me anymore."

"What will you do?"

Torbis knew that money wasn't a problem because there was no money anymore. But wouldn't people get bored if it all became automated?

"Walk my wolves. Grow vegetables in my garden. Spend time with my attachment. You know, whoever thought of this was really clever."

Ah. He thought so did he? If only he knew.

Torbis gazed though the window of his apartment. In the distance he could see the gently rolling hills covered in pink vegetation. It contrasted so well with the pale lemon sky. He was content. His apartment was comfortable and clean and tidy. He'd just had a new floor covering fitted. All was well.

There might have been a time a not so long ago when he would have been dissatisfied with this small apartment. A promotion in his work might mean a he could have afforded a bigger living space.

All that was finished now.

The terrible disease that had caused the Zenoton society to reject money left as suddenly as it had arrived. Exactly two years ago today there were suddenly no new cases. Zenotons stopped dying prematurely.

What would he do today? He had one meeting via his dataserve. He would take a hike in the hills afterwards and on the way back he would call into the selection centre and choose something delicious for an evening meal with Celestina. It was all good. It amazed him how quickly they had built and programmed enough droids to take over the menial tasks and some of the more skilled ones, leaving the Zenoton to do only what delighted them.

The dataserve buzzed. "Send," he commanded. Celestina. Then

her face was on the screen and his own was in the corner. He could see that both of them had locks glowing pink.

"Well?" he said.

"Yes. Of course, yes."

They both laughed. The meal this evening would certainly be a celebration. She had agreed to become his attachment.

"What do you think? Shall we take it?"

Celestina nodded. "It's perfect."

It was. The view from here was even better than the one from either of their current apartments. "Okay, I'll let them know we accept." Torbis was glad she liked it. Though they would never be forced to accept the first apartment they viewed he hadn't relished viewing apartment after apartment. What was the point anyway? They were all finished to the same high spec and all were guaranteed excellent views. And this was the optimum distance from the places where they would both have to attend the occasional meets. It had all the space they could need: nice open plan living space, a roomy bedroom, a spare bedroom and two small offices, so a workplace each. They even had two bathrooms. What more could they want?

As soon as he'd finished the call to the housing department he was a bit disturbed to find Celestina frowning.

He touched her arm. "What's the matter? I thought you liked it?"

"I do, I do. But this space is so large and all of our furniture is neutral in colour. It might look a bit cold, a bit drab?"

He could see what she meant.

"Well, shall we go and have a look at the stores? See if we can find something."

Celestina nodded. "Yes, maybe some colourful throws and cushions?"

The droid assistant trundled over with a few more cushions.

"I like that red and that turquoise," said Celestina. "But it needs something else as well."

She was right but Torbis couldn't think what it might be.

"Shall I fetch more assistance?" asked the droid.

Torbis nodded but before he could say "Yes please" the droid was on his way. Seconds later a Zenoton goods assistant was with them.

"I think we need another colour," said Celestina. "But we don't know what."

The Zenoton nodded. "I think I have just the thing."

He came back with a deep purple throw. Celestina gasped as she touched it. "It's so soft. And it shimmers."

"Yes. This is brand new material we've developed. The colour will stay vibrant. The texture will remain firm yet soft through a thousand laser cleans or water washes. You'll only have to replace it if you get fed up of the colour."

"I don't think there's any danger of that." Celestina held the soft material to her cheek. "I think that's it, then."

The assistant bowed slightly and put his hand together. "May I ask why you require these?"

Celestina's locks glowed pink. "We've just acquired a new apartment. There's so much space it looks a little cold."

The assistant smiled and his own locks twinkled a calm green. "Then you are of course most welcome to these items."

Torbis still couldn't believe how easy and how satisfying this all was. "How do we do it? How come there is enough for everyone and we keep it up to this standard?"

The assistant bowed again. "Because we've all learnt to practise gratitude since the virus left. And because we've continued to dream big."

Torbis smiled to himself. Yes, that was it. And he'd had a part in it all, hadn't he?

An Old Game for the New Normal

Dianne Stadhams

Bored by lock down? Want to play a game in the aftermath?

Then answer me this: What's simultaneously simple, strong, spectacular, secretive, significant and strategic?

Oh great – a word game! Does the answer start with an S word? I hear you ask.

Possibly but not probably.

So many choices. I hear you say.

You're smart so it shouldn't take too long.

Give us a clue or two. I hear you beg.

What's the fun in that? Well okay, since it's you, I'm happy to play.

CLUE 1

All languages have sayings about fame, most of them urging caution and advising the price paid is too high when balanced against the gains. All cultures have tales of famous folk who fell from the heights – from Humpty Dumpty to Marie Antoinette. Their bruises and broken bits testify in silence. But hey, who listens to mortal advice? There is always an outlier who proves someone can do it – maybe you?

Me – I can highly recommend celebrity status. Fame has offered me the Everest of perks – recognition, devotion, headlines, fear, respect – and the potential to travel the earth at my own pace, however with whomever.

Everyone wants to know everything about ME. What's not to love about that? Be honest! From zero to zenith in record time, I can hardly believe it. My image is universally recognised, though I avoid selfies. I've been front page news, headline television, the star of documentaries, top of the tweets and texts. Though I give no interviews I'm a living, global gangster god. No end in sight. I shower my fame like so many bats hanging down to pile on the pooh.

Got it yet?

Are you like… a footballer? A pop star? A reality show winner? you ask.

No, I say. But you all know my name whether I'm in your contact circle or not.

Black or white?

Irrelevant.

Male or female?

Gender neutral.

Woke or what?

Politically correctness is not important.

Confused… give us a clue?

Really. spoil sport? Well okay, since it's you.

CLUE 2

The Chinese say when a thing reaches its limits it must turn.

I don't have a problem with that adage. Of course, the decision becomes: in which direction should you turn?

Not my responsibility, I have to say. I go with the opportunities. Being a loner has never appealed. I don't flourish without others. I want to hang around with my own and venture forth into the great unknowns – wherever you decide to take me.

That's my definition of normal… old normal… new normal… whatever… there's not much difference.

However you might choose to play safe. Retreat. Isolate. Lock down. Peer out. One step at a time.

I advocate the grand plan. Go as far as you can. Pause only to admire the range of choice on offer and the number of players in the game. Life for me and you embraces so many chances to find fulfilment or failure. The potential is infectious like laughter… or malaria.

This is too big a challenge, I hear you say.

Lock down and share what you've found.

It's unprecedented.

That's the fun isn't it? A new challenge to consider.

That's not normal.

Define normal – yours or mine?
Give us a break. What's the answer?
Okay, as it's you I'll share a thing or two.
Whew – that's generous.
You reckon!

ANSWER

In the game of New Normal… venture out from behind your mask… rejoin the world in which you want to work and play. Da-da beat the drums, roll the dice and behold… all is revealed… a vaccine tale to keep you safe and sane.

Me… as a Covid-19 virus… will skip the celebrations. I am guaranteed my place in history… in perpetuity… if that is not a paradox from the days of old normal… for all men.

My marauding relatives applaud my celebrity status. They want to follow in my footsteps, handshakes, coughs and sneezes.

"Show me the way," cousin G4-strain-of-H1n1, potential, pandemic, influenza virus shouts.

I can but smirk. You can all be assured my new normal will be mutation… keep up, keep breathing and watch this space!

And Then…

Janet Howson

The thundering traffic.
Clamouring, claustrophobic, crowding, closeness.
Searing, smoke scarred, stolen sky.
Packed parks, people playing, posing, partying.
Bustling beaches, barbeques, browning, burning, basking bodies.
Restored restaurants, reinvented, rated, revisited, remembered, rowdy.
Pulsating pubs, pints, prosecco, pitchers, plenty.
Diaries, deadlines, dates, demands, departures, deletions.
Sports, stadiums, shouting, scoring, screaming.
Beauty benefits back.
Closeness, cuddles, caresses, chatting, carefree.
Education ensues, examinations, employment established earnings.
Lost lives lamented, longing, leaving, looking, loving.
  Furloughing Finished.
  Quarantine Quashed.
  Sanitising Stopped.
  Covid Cancelled.
Until the next time…

Real and Unreal

Mari Phillips

Switch on computer
check the log-in, is this real?
Full hearts, empty chairs.

The funeral passed,
a minister and webcast.
No mourners, no hugs.

Words, prayers and music,
memories unspoken by
virtual mourners.

No Wake, just What's App?
Or was it Zoom? A real death
in an unreal world.

Post Lockdown Limbo

Mari Phillips

Go to work,
but avoid the train.
If you must take a bus
wear a mask.

Feral kids in gardens,
interrupting Zoom meetings or
fixed in front of screens.

Small shops, dead streets
and one-way systems.
Visit the pub for distanced pints
on Super Saturday
or was it Sardine Saturday?

Hayrick hair shorn,
but no spas or toes.
Keep up the Pilates or yoga,
the gym's still not open.
No theatre, choirs,
but football behind closed doors.

Take a holiday – by plane?
No way.
My body's willing but my head's not straight,
stuck in a post lockdown limbo.

The New Normal

Gill James

John switched off the TV. That was it then. The pubs were shut. People who could work from home were asked to do just that. People like him, over seventy years old, were told to stay at home. They'd also said don't use public transport. For goodness sake – that's one of the reasons he'd chosen to live here. His house was as near to a least five bus routes so buses came every few minutes even on a Sunday. Wasn't that supposed to help save the planet? And he couldn't go to the pub. Darn!

"Bloody over reaction," he muttered to himself. "It's just an excuse to keep us oldies out of the way."

He went into the kitchen, filled the kettle, and switched it on. Well at least he could still make a cuppa. How long would that last though? How long before everything broke down and the electricity ran out? Would it be like in one of those novels about dystopias he liked to read? He'd better keep away from those for a bit. Real life was getting a lot more bizarre than fiction. But he didn't want to camp. He couldn't imagine a life without light at the flick of a switch, heat that you only noticed if wasn't there and people who came and took the rubbish away every week. He'd worked hard all his life for this. Why shouldn't he enjoy it? Surely they could get it fixed? Or were they too idle these days? He remembered then what his late wife Sandra had once said. She'd been an immunologist and he'd asked her why they couldn't immunise against cancer or Aids, or HIV.

"It's not always straightforward," she'd said. "Sometimes developed vaccines can do more harm than good. That happened with something they tried on cats recently." And there'd been nothing for her. Lung cancer had taken her off within six weeks of diagnosis. She'd never smoked in her life. How had that happened? Was the air so badly polluted? Had it been because of passive smoking when she was younger? He'd smoked when they first got married but he'd given it up when the children were born. Was it his fault?

The kettle boiled. Good grief he hoped he didn't get the darned thing. It looked nasty. Besides, he was a mere seventy-one. He was looking forward to at least another twenty years.

As he drank his cuppa he looked through his diary. Well, pretty well all of that would be cancelled. U3A meetings. U3A had said they wouldn't risk any physical meetings for the foreseeable future. Dentist appointment. Dentists couldn't operate as usual because of the aerosol effect. It never stopped them when TB or Spanish 'flu was around did it? Or did they just not blow things around so much then? Theatre trips. He had several theatre trips booked. And what about the various committees he was on? What would happen with them? Most of the other committee members were the same age as him so he guessed he wouldn't miss anything. Could they perhaps do everything via email?

After he'd finished his tea he went on-line. He found emails from the theatres offering refunds or vouchers for events once they were open again. One blatantly asked if they could just keep the money. John paused to think about that for a few minutes. Well why not? In fact why didn't they all do that? He'd never get the time back and the money was spent now. He wanted them to open again once all of this was over. And why were all of these people offering all of this free on-line entertainment? They ought at least to ask for a donation. He would give gladly.

Oh, he needed to sort out food. He'd get it delivered. That should be easy enough. But good grief, Tesco's and Morrisons didn't have any slots until three weeks hence. Sainsbury's was four weeks. Even Waitrose was going to be fifteen days. The only one who could oblige with a slot in five days was Asda. That would have to do. He'd never shopped at Asda before but they seemed to have all the same goods as the others.

The doorbell rang. He opened it and stepped back. It was the young woman from the house opposite. "We're still working and we can get out," she said. She put an envelope down on the bonnet of his car. "Both Sam and I work for the NHS so if there's anything you need, just give us a ring. Our numbers are in there."

Of course, yes, they both worked at the local health centre. "Would you be able to pick my prescription from the chemist's? It's usually the last week of the month."

"Of course we will. Just give us a ring once it's ready."

People were being so kind. It would be extra work for them even though the chemist was attached to the health centre. No doubt there would be queues with fewer staff working and social distancing being enforced.

So that was everything sorted. But how was he going to keep himself occupied? Well he had plenty of recorded television to watch. And tons of books to read He had twenty paperbacks in the bedroom waiting to be read and goodness knows how many books on his Kindle. Then there was that piano. It was an antique grand and dominated the room. He hadn't touched it since Sandra died. Perhaps he could take it up again. He played a scale. Yes, it was more or less in tune. He started to play a piece that he knew quite well and noticed the jigsaw puzzles that sat unopened on the bookshelves. He shouldn't be bored, then after all.

The phone rang one morning.

"Hello," he answered.

"Hi John, it's Colin. Have you heard of Zoom?"

"No what's that?

"It's a free video-conferencing thingy. We could carry on our philosophy group with it. Fancy giving it a try?"

"Okay then." John wasn't really so sure. He liked his computer well enough but he hated having to learn new things.

"Good. I'll send you an email with instructions."

It proved to be easier than he'd have thought. Soon he and most of his friends from the U3A Philosophy Group were 'meeting' twice a month on-line instead of the once a month in person. Other groups soon sprang up. And all of those committees he was on also used the clever little app. Attendance at such meetings was better than normal; nobody had got anywhere else to go and it saved a drive or hopping on a bus. They mostly used the free version, which meant a welcome five minute gap after forty minutes – enough time for a visit to the lav or to make a cuppa – and also guaranteed that no meeting lasted more than an hour and a half.

He even managed to keep in touch with his daughter and grandchildren.

"It's good isn't it, this?" he said to Sally after he'd watched Harry and Elena put on a clown performance for him. "Not, of course, as good as seeing you for real but better than nothing, hey?"

Sally had laughed. "Yes, and they've had something like this for school though I will be glad when they can go back. They're missing their friends."

"How's your work going?"

"Not bad. I like working from home. I hope they'll let me carry on afterwards. But it's difficult home-schooling them at the same time."

"I'll do a bit, if you like, via Zoom."

"That would be great, Dad."

And so John found himself teaching again.

He became so busy that he began to wonder how he'd ever managed to go out anywhere before – just like not long after he'd retired he'd wondered how he'd ever had time to work. He began to relish the days he had no Zoom meetings. He'd got a lot of other things to do as well.

He got into quite a routine. Mornings he spent doing housework and admin. Afternoons were for the piano, the garden and jigsaw puzzles. Evenings were for TV and books. It was all beginning to work rather well.

John found another delight. He missed his beloved theatre but there were some very interesting things popping up on-line. Most of them were free. They ought to charge for them. When some of them invited you to donate or pay what you could afford he was quite generous. He enjoyed political debates, theatre performances and interviews with well-known people. How could anybody complain of being bored? And there was often an added bonus here; you got to see into the homes of the rich and famous and best of all got to see what they had on their bookshelves. It also occurred to him that more people were ‘attending’ these events on-line than meeting rooms had for capacity in real life. The government was beginning to get concerned about the economy. But weren’t these on-line providers missing a trick here? “Paywall, paywall,” he muttered to himself and occasionally shouted at the television. But what a joy it was to watch *Question Time* with a socially distanced panel and minus the idiotic audience members who hadn’t a clue what they were talking about and who clapped like performing seals when somebody said something pretentious.

His piano playing improved no end and he could now even play a few of the Chopin pieces without looking at the music. When he did need to use the sheet music, he no longer had to stop and think what the dots meant. His fingers glided over the keys and the elegant but dominating piece of furniture was justifying its existence. If only Sandra could see him now.

The weather was sunnier than he’d ever remembered up here in Rainy City. On some afternoons he sat out in the garden. The flowers bloomed well. There were more bees and butterflies than ever. He was sure there were more birds singing this year. Or was that just because he had more time to notice? Or because he could hear them better – the main road, a block away, was quieter than normal? The air was sweeter as well. You hardly ever saw a plane making a mess of the sky anymore. And nature had been coming back: mountain goats in Llandudno, wild boars in Barcelona and in his own northern suburban garden one morning a crane.

Then one day it was on the radio: they hadn’t needed to use fossil fuels to power an electricity station since March.

He hoped that some of these good changes that had come in would continue after the lockdown was lifted.

But the government continued to worry about the economy. They had to get the country moving again, they said. John was torn. He was convinced that the economy stood a better chance of recovering if they dealt with the disease properly first. But what did he know? He was just a retired primary school teacher. Okay, so his maths was competent enough but he wasn't exactly the greatest economist, was he? He didn't quite trust this lot. He had a feeling that they were self-serving but it was difficult to be sure. He talked to his son Jeff about it.

"Well, the kids'll be back a school next-week. Part-time." He rolled his eyes. "Different days. So I'll still be working from home."

"Isn't that better than going into the office though?"

"Well, yes. And actually they're getting more out of me because I'm not spending so much time commuting."

"You're happy about them being back at school?"

"I don't know what to think, Dad. They're young and they're strong, I suppose. And I think their teachers have pretty well got it figured out. We'll just have to see."

John was glad he didn't have to go out. Masks, that was the other thing. They really made people look spooky. He didn't like wearing one himself. He'd tried it when he'd had to go to the health centre for a routine blood test. It made his specs mist up and he couldn't breathe properly.

"You should try a washable cotton mask," one of the ladies from the philosophy group had said. "Wash your specs in soapy water and put them over your mask." She'd send him some cotton ones she'd made. He'd tried one of them out at home. And it worked. Not that he had any intention of going out again if he could help it. No, he would rather wait until everything was completely back to normal. He just didn't like seeing other people in masks. Still if he had to go out he now knew what to do.

Then he got the email from Specsavers. Yes, his eye test was two months overdue and yes, his eyes did feel a bit strained. All that screen work perhaps. He probably needed a new prescription and some new frames would not go amiss.

The day came for the appointment at the opticians. John was torn. Should he take the car? What if he couldn't get a parking space? It wasn't all that far to walk but it was uphill. And he wasn't sure of the timing. He didn't want to be late. Or too early for that matter. In the end he decided on the bus, even though the use of public transport was discouraged. He allowed about an hour. It only took fifteen minutes from his front door to the centre of town normally. He couldn't be sure what sort of timetable the buses would be running to. He had his mask and white cotton gloves. It would probably be all right.

It was almost like old times, waiting for the bus. A woman about the same age as him arrived at the bus stop. She nodded at him and stood a decent two metres away. And just like in the days before the lockdown he had to wait less than five minutes for the bus.

It was a familiar double-decker but it was different inside. Half the seats had tape over them. He and the woman were the only passengers. There was hardly any traffic on the roads. He was incredibly early. He guessed he wouldn't be welcome inside the shopping centre yet, so he sat in the gardens next to the bus station. He was a little surprised at how much he enjoyed watching people going about their normal business. It was nowhere as busy as it would normally be but there were enough people there to make it interesting.

The visit to the optician went smoothly. It was very much as normal though he was asked to use the hand sanitizer as soon as he reported to reception. "And you're feeling fit and well today?" asked the young woman behind the desk. She was obviously used to making herself clear even with a covering over her face. There were fewer people in the store than normal and he hardly had to wait at all. Yes, it was decided, he did need a new prescription. "You're sure it's all right to touch these?" he said, when he was invited to try on some new frames.

"Oh yes sir," said the young lad. "We clean each set of frames very carefully after they've been touched."

As he went out of the store a woman and a young boy stepped aside. She was wearing a very pretty floral mask that also covered her neck. The boy had a rather dramatic skull and cross-bones on his. John's eyes met the woman's. He could tell she was smiling, despite the mask. Perhaps he could get used to them after all.

He decided to walk home. He stopped and sat down for a while at the park that was halfway between his house and the town centre. It was very pleasant and the café was even serving take away drinks. He decided to indulge himself with a cup of tea. He got chatting to the man and woman sitting at the next bench. Perhaps there was life after lockdown after all.

John still tried to stay at home as much as possible. His routines were disrupted, however. There were now fewer Zoom meetings as his U3A buddies started visiting relations and taking small holidays again. Sally and Jeff were still a little too far away, but he did risk the swimming pool. It was bizarre turning up in his swimmers and going home wet. At least, though, it was nice having the pool almost to himself and the few other people who were there kept to the rule of staying five metres apart.

As soon as he was home again he got out of his wet things and took a welcome shower. Then he put on the kettle. As he waited for it to boil he watched the squirrels in the garden. Now, they were good at social distancing. They were two metres apart all right – which to them was more like twelve metres or more would be for humans. Of course they had to get close now and then or there'd be no more squirrels.

He switched on the radio as he made his tea. He was just in time to catch a news bulletin. So, the death rate was the lowest it had been in a five year period. Not only did the virus seem to be more or less under control but fewer people were dying of other things. The expert thought it was partly to do with social distancing and partly to do with the cleaner air.

As he sipped his tea John hoped that life could carry on just like it was right now. He'd operate mainly from home. He'd carry on enjoying all the new on-line activities he'd found. He'd go out occasionally and enjoy the spaces that were far less crowded than they used to be. He'd relish the fresher air. He'd just have to get used to the masks.

Conditioned

Dawn DeBraal

How does she stop looking at someone approaching her without her evil eye look of daggers, directed at the person not practicing social distancing? How does she grab a door without thinking of the thousand other people who touched it before her? And masks. What about masks? The vaccine was supposed to give them back their courage. But she still prayed that they hadn't given themselves some form of cancer or Alzheimer's disease somewhere down the line from taking the vaccine.

Dorothy wondered about those in the flu pandemic in 1918. How long did it take before they forgot the fear and the anxiety?

As she watched an old television program, something that aired twenty years ago, a cordless phone rang. The woman on the screen picked it up and used her teeth to pull up the antenna.

"Hello?" the woman said. Dorothy was near vomiting. That woman just put a metal phone antenna in her mouth and pulled it up with her teeth. Ten years ago, this wouldn't have phased her a bit, but now she was a germaphobe.

The doorbell rang. Dorothy's first instinct was to hide. Let the postal person stand out there and rot for all she cared. She was not answering the door, for there was still another disease out there on the horizon. She hated her neighbour, who she watched carry in three huge packages of toilet paper. Why? Why would a single woman need ninety-six rolls of toilet paper? All the conditioning she'd done over the last two years could not be undone overnight. Dorothy still carried hand sanitizer in her pocket and had a pull key thingy that opened doors or pushed keypads with no touch. And her business, making face masks. Now, what was she going to do to make extra money in her reclining years? How do you unlearn everything you learned to do now that the pandemic had passed? There were only a few people who refused to be vaccinated; perhaps there was enough of a market to peddle her masks. The world was changed. Maybe not for the better.

She moved out to her garage, opened the door, started up her car. She was on a trip to the grocery store. Her courage faltered when she pulled up at the market. It was packed. The fear she felt was palpable, but those in power deemed the virus controlled. Did she walk into the store, unmasked with no wipes to clean the cart? She watched. There were a few hold outs, still clinging to the safety of their face masks. But for the most part, people were going commando. How could the world change overnight?

Dorothy grabbed her cell phone. She had her credit card on that now, so she wouldn't have to touch the dirty keypad. Simply tap her phone to an electronic base, it sucked all her information with its passing and paid her bill. She was paranoid about losing her phone but more paranoid about touching those keypads and using that disgusting pen to sign her name.

"You can do this," she told herself as she started to walk into the store but soon found herself back inside her car. She grabbed her mask off the rear-view mirror. She wasn't ready yet. It just was too good to be true.

She wiped down her cart with a sanitary wipe. For good measure, she did it again. She looked at her phone list and started making her way through the grocery store, picking out her fruits and vegetables. Without thinking, she backed into a man.

"I'm so very sorry," they both exclaimed. Dorothy back-pedalled to the other side of the produce aisle.

"It was my fault. I wasn't paying attention," Dorothy said and resumed her shopping. The man looked like a nice person. He was also wearing a mask. Did that mean he had some underlying medical issues? Or, was he a diehard non-believer like she was? Dorothy turned the corner and selected some canned goods and noodles. The nice man rounded the corner; she kept looking back. She was afraid as he got closer to her cart. What happened to the rules? Were they all gone now? She trotted around the corner to the next aisle. She didn't need anything. Perhaps she could make her way a few aisles ahead of the man. They were in the same shopping pattern. She needed to break the cycle. Dorothy went to the meat section. She tried to find the smallest roast, a package with one or two chicken legs in it. Why did they pack meat like it was for a family of five? Why couldn't she just by one leg? She sighed, picking up the package with three legs. She would eat one and freeze the rest. It just seemed too hard to ask them to break up the set.

Dorothy finished her shopping. She used her key thingy to punch in her phone number, to get the discount coupons. She waved her phone across the top of the machine. It sucked the money out of her bank account by some miracle and paid the store. Though she was against plastic bags, she stood passively as they piled in her groceries. She longed for the day she could bring in her reusable bags so she could tell the plastic bag industry to stick it. They were building an environmental menace in the ocean. Dorothy put the groceries in her trunk of her car, unlocking the driver's door when she looked up. She saw the mystery shopper man. It was her neighbour from a few doors down. My, he had lost a lot of weight.

"Dorothy! It's me, Ken!" the man called out to her. He was across from her car, two cars down.

"Hello, neighbour, I didn't recognize you!" She smiled; they were at least thirty feet apart.

"Yes, well, you know I got the virus. My wife Eileen died, and I lost fifty pounds. I am feeling much better now."

"I am so sorry about Eileen. How long has it been?"

"About a year. Thank you for your kind words." Dorothy felt sorry for the man.

"Say, I had to buy three chicken legs. Would you like to have a picnic outside for dinner tonight?" Dorothy couldn't believe she was saying this. She wasn't ready to have Ken in her house, but she thought about doing chicken on the grill with a little social distancing. Besides, they were both still practicing to be safe. She didn't need to worry about him.

"I would love to. I will bring a bottle of wine. I think white will go well with chicken, correct?" Dorothy giggled, batting her eyes at Ken. Smiling, she drove out of the parking lot. She and Ken had come through a storm. Maybe there could be life and love, after a pandemic.

Plasticus Quercus

Pam Pottinger

In 2020

Grown on a whim, with seeds found at the back of a drawer, tomato plants have taken over his window ledge, megalithic in stature, they defy the odds, to flourish in used milk cartons. They are, he thinks, in danger of outgrowing their own strength.

"It's like an underwater cavern in here," Youssoup, (Soup for short) says from the doorway.

Alex looks. "Yeh, I'm going to try and get some more soil from somewhere."

"Like steal it from a park you mean?"

"Na, need too much... need to get them outside too, somewhere they can be in the sunshine all day."

His phone pings. His mum. S*kylark*... an attachment reveals a picture of a tiny dot in the sky. Sometimes her messages make him smile. Sometimes not. This one is somewhere in between. The recent lockdown has made him prone to more than the usual amount of anxiety. He mourns the loss of green, big skies and open spaces.

"This place is nothing but a bloody concrete..."

"London is a city, that is why..." Soup, ever literal, explains.

"I know, I know all that, but it gets me down sometimes. That plaque near the entrance gates, the one they screwed to the wall, the one that says *Providing better communities through carefully nurtured spaces*, makes me feel angry."

"You can't be angry at a piece of metal."

Oh couldn't he? He knew what the view from his window was. Plasticus Quercus, the half dead oak, a thin rectangle of yellowed grass, a three legged bench. Incapably on its side. It was all dysfunctional.

"So you think building one thousand flats in one acre of ground is a good thing?"

"No, but it is as it is and we have to try and make the best of it."

"They ought to be prosecuted for telling lies."

He found The Best Top Soil Company, listed in a local directory. It was unfortunate that they only sold by the ton but, well he'd just grow more stuff that was all. Could be good. Green beans, herbs, potatoes, strawberries – when he was little he and his brothers would complain about always having strawberries for pudding. He pressed the button on £150 worth of soil. Savings gone. Whatever.

The next day, out running, he saw two men carrying a bathtub out of a house. Perfect. "Hey, are you chucking that away?"

"Leaks…" one of them said as they continued down the path toward its final heave ho.

"Wait a minute, I don't want it for a bath."

"Still cost you a tenner…"

"Okay," said Alex who couldn't abide quibbling. But also knowing the man would wish he'd asked fifteen. All he had to worry about now was how to get it back home.

In his pocket his phone rang as well as pinged.

Soup said. "There is a mountain of soil outside the gates, people are complaining they cannot get in."

His Mum wrote. Golden Plover… my lucky day, how's yours going?

Soup said. "Can you hear me?"

Alex smiled. "Actually I was just going to ring you…" Yep, so far so good.

He rescued more stuff from the skip. Plant pots, a withered spider plant, a clip on spotlight, a kitchen chair with four good legs and a half decent seat. When Soup arrived he raised an eyebrow. Even for best friends steering a bath full of rubbish round lampposts, between parking meters, multitudes of cats (all purposely out to trip him up) could test things a bit.

Alex said. "I'll count to three and then we go for it, okay."

The bath was heavy. Soup thought he was going to have a permanent dip in his back after this. It was further to go than it was to come. He couldn't ask to rest because he was frightened he'd show himself up by not being able to pick it up again. He tried counting steps, cars, people. There were not enough of the latter to take his mind off the pain of wearing a bath upon his shoulder. By the time they got to the soil mountain he was past caring. About anything.

The caretaker wasn't. "This yours matey?"

"Erm yeh, they said it wouldn't be here for a week."

"You'll have to get it shifted before then. Can't just leave it there can ye?"

Alex turned to Soup. "We need a wheelbarrow…"

Soup walked away laughing. "I'll throw you the washing bowl."

How many washing up bowls of soil does it take to move a ton of the stuff? Anyone?

He ferried to the middle of the car park, piling soil around the base of Plasticus Quercus, where, he tried his best to stop it spilling over into the surrounding parking spaces. It was one of those thankless tasks, as it constantly erupted in a flow of mini earthquakes. There was simply too much of it. He'd been at it for hours too. His back, arms and neck, all felt as if they would break and so head down, not seeing the sky, all dusky with the promise of stars, he went to join Soup in their flat. He'd worry about the curtain twitchers tomorrow.

In the end the curtain twitchers decided against complaint. It wasn't every day a bath got dragged around the car park. Or soil in such abundance it looked as if the earth had opened up. No. they would not complain. They wanted to know what next. Wait, watch, see.

Mid-morning someone shouted. "You got soil down there enough for me garden boy?"

"How much do you want?" He called back.

"Enough for a plant pot."

"Okay, do you want to come and get some?"

"It's me legs," she said.

"What floor are you?"

"Tenth if you don't count the laundry area."

He filled the bowl and started climbing. When he got there she was holding a plant pot ready. It had a split down the side. She was too old for him to say anything.

He went back downstairs, got one of the pots he'd taken from the skip. Went back up.

"What are you going to put in it?" He asked as he filled it for her.

"Spider plant, now I got me a pot, I'm gonna get me a spider plant."

They looked at each other steadily while he waited for her next question.

"You not gotta a spider plant have you?"

"It'll need a bit of TLC."

"Is my speciality, I got five children all growed fine and gone."

He counted the steps, multiplied them by two for each time he'd gone up and three for each time he'd gone back up. 6,480 steps and he still wasn't finished. His phone pinged, *neighbour passed me this...* picture of honeysuckle cutting... *cheered me no end.* Right he thought. Right.

The next day he had a small queue waiting – two more requests for soil, a question about growing potatoes and someone wanting to know if they could garden too. A child with a dog watched him from a distance but said nothing. He doled out the soil, googled potatoes, said yes, if you want to garden, I'm sure that's okay. Ignored the child, but put a hand out to the dog as he passed by.

The day after that he found a flask of tea and a couple of biscuits wrapped in a piece of kitchen roll, hanging from a branch of the tree, which, he noticed, had tiny buds on it. Not Plasticus after all then, just Quercus. Oak.

Eventually the caretaker comes to his door. "What is it?" Alex asks worried he's gone too far with the cracked Belfast sink a friend has given him.

"Just letting you know you've got another ton of soil coming, be here tomorrow."

"Eh...?" said Alex. "Eh...!"

"And a workman coming to build some containers, just let him know where yer want them and he'll box in the bath while he's here."

"I don't understand, I mean…"

"It don't exactly look pretty that bath do it?"

"But…"

"Someone's seen what yer doin', now council's told me to get more stuff. Yer'll have ter let me know if you need money for more plants." He leaves.

Soup stands by the window. "Look." He beckons Alex across.

A man is sitting on a chair at the side of his bath, which is now rampant green with plants. He's not doing anything, just sitting, reading a book.

"It is the aftermath of your efforts." Soup doesn't always get his words right.

Alex looks at him. Says. "Yeh. Not quite sure aftermath is the word you're looking for though Soup. Aftermath means…"

"I know what aftermath means Alex. I have seen it." He has, in all the guises a broken land has to offer. "But this is new for me, it gives me hope."

In 2030

Alex knows this about the place he once lived. It is now a model to follow for inner city areas, plants hang from balconies like jewels, birds sing the residents awake. A man, once a child with a dog, tends the gardens and shows visitors around. Plasticus Quercus no longer stands alone, apple and plum flank his sides. His acorns are gathered to grow on and plant far and wide. Chance has caused one to grow within a mile of Alex's home, his mother passes it every day and often sends pictures of its progress. The plaque that so annoyed Alex has been taken down.

In Case I Forget

Hannah Retallick

23/7/20

Lockdown is easing off in Wales. Throughout these uncertain and difficult times (what an overused phrase!), I've realised how many blessings can go unnoticed in our normal busyness. I'm not an ungrateful person; I enjoy the 'little things' and write a daily gratitude journal. I have a new appreciation for life though. I'd like to say I'll never forget these feelings, but I might, so that's why I'm writing them down. These are a few of the things I'd like to remember: a funny mix of big/generalised and smaller/personal things.

I want to remember the new friendships formed with neighbours. When we were required to stay close to home and only go out for exercise, people connected more – smiling, saying hello, and getting into conversation. It felt like a happier estate, with a strengthened community spirit.

I want to remember how blessed I was to be safe and well at home. *Safe at home, not stuck at home*.

I want to remember the importance of taking care of mental health. Lockdown has had a severe impact. From what I've noticed, it's been a mixture of people finding life much easier and finding it much harder, and sometimes swinging between the two. I'm introverted and don't mind spending a lot of time by myself… until I really *need* a cuddle. Friends and family still looked out for me though. I'm grateful for that and I hope I did the same for others.

I want to remember the valuable time that could be used for jobs such as cleaning, tidying, and DIY. I think I saw a neighbour wash his car two days in a row… but maybe I imagined it!

I want to remember that it wasn't big parties or international travel I craved during isolation, but to watch Friends with my dad and aunt, to give my besties big hugs, and to stroll 'down vill' to… oh, I don't know, buy a stamp from the Post Office.

I want to remember the wonderful adaptability and flexibility of humans in an emergency. We're a creative bunch.

I want to remember how to wash my hands properly. Ok, I didn't need to learn that – Mum drilled it into us at a young age. She was in her element! But yes, wash your hands properly and don't cough and sneeze over everyone – sorry to ruin your fun.

I want to remember how blessed we are to have access to the internet and a wealth of technology, allowing us to stay connected when we can't be physically close. All sorts of support groups sprung up. And Zoom… wow, that became all the rage.

I want to remember how artists/creatives were essential in keeping our spirits up, entertaining us, and expressing emotions. They might not be given the title of 'essential workers'… but where would we be without them?

I want to remember the time by myself, not feeling any social pressure to see people, and having the space to be alone with my thoughts… even if that got too much at times. I've never been more aware of the cacophony (mm, great word) of strangeness in my head!

I want to remember the time I spent with Mum in isolation. We did some whacky fun stuff, and no one got hurt… even in the whimsical wooden-spoon duel! Dancing to *Jailhouse Rock* in the living room isn't weird – I stand by that.

I want to remember walking along a usually busy road and hearing no traffic. It might have been slightly eerie, but the natural world had the chance to strengthen its voice.

I want to remember the Facebook posts and memes (yes, really) that brought smiles and laughter. Humour is a tonic.

I want to remember how invaluable the NHS is, as well as all the keyworkers who had to keep going throughout lockdown – medical staff, emergency services, shelf stackers, refuse collectors etc. Thank you for keeping the country running, and well done for gritting your teeth when people around you were constantly referring to 'spare time' and even 'boredom'!

I want to remember how privileged we are to have a garden. I don't take full advantage of ours normally, but I can only imagine how difficult it must have been not to have one, particularly in the early stages of lockdown.

I want to remember the opportunity many people had to take up new hobbies, reignite their love of old hobbies, or work on their health regimes. I learnt some jive steps. No, I'm not showing you.

I want to remember stepping back from 'modern life'. It was like hitting the reset button.

I want to remember leaving the house on a lovely day and thinking, *Despite everything, this could not be any more gorgeous. Despite everything, the sun is shining. Despite everything, the birds are singing.*

I want to remember the wonderous thing that is toilet paper… but I doubt I'll forget that one! It was crazy, wasn't it? (Don't stockpile, people. It ain't cool.)

What are some of the things *you* want to remember from this time?

First Person

John Guest

Actually, it was the third wave that did all the damage.

The second wave had been bad enough, though it had been a long time coming. Somewhat ironically nineteen months after the dire predictions of disaster when everyone, even the cynical realists, had thought they were safe. When even the Swedish scientists had given the thumbs up. Of course, by then all the normal people and normal things were…

Well, back to normal.

The virus had been part of history. Ancient history according to these rapidly changing times. Families and friends were together again. International travel was booming. The worldwide economy was beginning to bounce back. Trump had proclaimed the Wall Street Surge as the greatest comeback since Lazarus. And the new Hollywood blockbuster The C Word, starring Matt Damon and Meryl Streep, had hit the high street to rave reviews.

Then the second wave struck.

Worse than the first. Harder. Longer. Millions had died. Of course, the world was prepared for another pandemic. The processes were in place, the equipment still available. The problem was they were not prepared enough. Not enough for something this big. Not for something this overwhelming.

The leaders that were left when the virus had done its deadly work called a virtual summit. A meeting of minds to think the unthinkable, plan the radical. Organise the beleaguered nations of the world into some kind of coalition for rebuilding. Out of the shattered remnants of society a tottering new civilization began to emerge like green shoots through the blackened chaos of a tortured landscape. Life could find a way.

And then the third wave struck.

Adam shut his laptop. Enough for now. He needed to eat.

He dispensed exactly 400ml of liquid from the water purifying unit and pressed two buttons on the hydro. Plenty of pizza left – ha ha! Two minutes later he was munching his way through yet another pepperoni and mushroom.

Adele was playing through the system; the air-con was a tad too high. Adam kicked off his slippers and settled down to another boxed set. There was nothing else to watch since all the media had shut down four months ago.

BBC World service had been the last to succumb. God only knew where they'd been broadcasting from. The news had been unremittingly dire. The third wave had finished the planet. Yes, that was what had really done the damage.

First, all the children died. Mercifully quickly but nonetheless relentlessly. And no treatment, no protection, no antidote could save them. All that had been learned from wave one and wave two had helped them not at all. Every child under eighteen without exception in every nation across the globe died before the month was out. Yet the grief for their passing was itself overwhelmed as the virus mutated and swept through the elderly and vulnerable and swallowed them up also.

By this time every system was down, every response thwarted and the fabric of society unravelled like ripped cotton. The strength of the third wave virus was matched only by its speed and all humanity now faced the certainty of extinction. The religious prayed, the scientists toiled, the politicians talked, the billionaires burrowed.

All to no avail.

Adam paused the drama and dropped his plate in the garbage chute. He had been left. Alone. Untouched. Unaffected.

No. Not unaffected. Not unaffected at all. The last person of seven billion in the ultimate lockdown. Socially distanced by 24, 901 miles.

When they'd set up the Experimental National Department for Testing and Investigating Multiple Ecosystems nearly six years ago he'd been one of a dozen Prediction Analysts in the somewhat sceptical science of forecasting future trends in pandemic statistics. Not that it had done them much good. He'd seen the trends but even he didn't believe them. Too much to take in. Too overwhelming to contemplate. He'd shared it with the others of course and they'd passed it higher. But even before the response came in, the sickness began.

And the deaths.

And Adam was alone. None of the disaster movies had prepared him for this. The blow on blow of death on death. Relentless. Unavoidable. Pointless.

Pointless.

Adam stared gloomily at the face peering at him from above his spotless sink. Hair cut. Teeth brushed. Chin shaved. Smartly laundered shirt. Glass of cool clean water in one hand. Tablets in the other.

First person. Singular.

And then, like the Clarion of Hope at the very last end of the world…

His mobile rang.

The Dusk Walkers

Henry Lewi

Did you notice sometimes out of the corner of your eye, sometimes in the shadows, the number of people who were out in the early hours of the morning, usually alone very occasionally in pairs? They kept to the shadows, silent and watching. Both Men and Women any age, all with bright shining eyes. If you approach them, they'll quickly and silently walk away, their only distinguishing features are their eyes. Who are they? What are they watching? What do they want? And what do they do?

It all began during the Virus lockdown in 2020. I had returned to help out at the local hospital where I'd worked as a surgeon for the previous 25 years. Although retired I responded to the request for retirees to volunteer to help out. My role was simple; it was to check on patients who'd been discharged from hospital or those who'd reported mild symptoms of the viral disease to their GPs. After contacting many patients, I became aware that some were reporting severe symptoms of recurrent persistent eye pain and a hypersensitivity to light or as we medics like to call it – Photophobia. I dully filled in the contact forms highlighting the symptoms described but during the height of the epidemic everyone was far too busy to comment.

After working in the hospital for about a month I tested positive for the virus but had no symptoms. However, a couple of weeks later I started to experience severe eye pain, and sensitivity to light. The pain was so severe I couldn't sleep but wasn't tired despite preferring the night hours to sit outside in the garden, doing little more than listen to audiobooks or the news.

Over the next few weeks the pain became less but the light sensitivity remained, interestingly my night vision improved so much that it seemed on many an occasion night became day. I found it difficult to go out in the bright daylight without sunglasses and my vision became clearer and crisper so much so that I had to discard my glasses that I always wore full time. The only problem was that I seemed to have a number of floaters in both my eyes.

As lockdown was eased, I managed to get an appointment at my optician's who confirmed that my vision was now perfect, the short-sightedness and severe astigmatism had completely reversed, but he was troubled by the changes in the eye which he jokingly stated – "If I didn't know better I'd say that you've got gold flakes in your eyes, which is why they look bright and shiny – I've never seen that before! Look I'll arrange for you to see one of the guys at Moorefield's Eye Hospital – I'm sure there's nothing to worry about at least you don't have to buy any glasses!"

At Moorefield's the consultant was puzzled and called in one of his colleagues to have a look, then another, and another and finally the professor was asked to have a look. Nobody came up with an answer, so I was asked to stay in 'for a number of tests' as they put it. I was given a nice private room and was subjected to a whole battery of 'tests' including scans, bloods, numerous eye examinations, and visits by numerous Ophthalmic Surgeons, Neurologists and a couple of doctors who introduced themselves as Metabolic Specialists. I must have given a pint and a half of blood and the conclusion at the end of this? Yup I had deposits of gold flakes in my eyes – why? It must be a consequence of the virus infection they said – How? Well here's the outline as I can remember – There's a series of enzymes in the body classified as cytochrome P450 that has a huge range of functions which include binding heavy metals to form what's called a metallo-enzyme. We all have a bit of gold in our bodies notably around the heart, in the joints and in our nerves. Somehow the Viral infection subtly altered the function of the cytochrome P450 which allowed it to leach out the gold from its normal sites and for some reason deposited it in the eyes. Jokingly they said that maybe this was the basis of the *Goose that Laid the Golden Egg* story? Really! So, what next? I asked – Well – pause – We don't really know, but yours is not the first – we've now heard of many similar cases throughout the country and from all over Europe – someone has even coined the name 'Goldeneye Syndrome'. What next – we don't know, but it would seem that the condition should, emphasizing the SHOULD, stabilize, as there is only a small amount of gold in the body that can be deposited. Stay out of the sun, wear sunglasses, eat a healthy diet, and we'll keep a regular and close eye on you.

So it was, the days turned into weeks, I avoided the daylight hours and lived my life in the dusk and night and on occasion I would meet someone in the shadows with the same problem, you can identify us by the fact that we wear sunglasses at night or by our shining metallic eyes.

It was all going OK till the news broke on TV with the exclusive, titled – *They Carry a Fortune in Their Eyes*.

Now I hear that people with Goldeneye, or even anyone wearing sunglasses are being hunted for their eyes, and I can't go out anymore.

There are no more Dusk Walkers around.

Where have they all gone?

Where can I go?

Bert's Choice

Susan A Eames

The last thing Bert remembered was his wife scolding him for going out to the shops without his mask. He always said she'd be the death of him instead of the virus.

And then he remembered: the virus was finally under control.

He heard his wife again, "It's only under control if we remain alert and wear our masks, you idiot."

Bert sighed. He was standing in a queue that seemed to stretch into infinity. It was going to take a long time to reach the source.

A voice interrupted his musings.

"Good morning, Bert. Name's Austin and it's my pleasure to serve."

A man holding a clip board stood before him. "Thought you'd appreciate a bit of queue jumping." Austin winked at Bert. "So, how do you want to go back?"

"Back?"

"This new to you then?"

"Why, of course it's new…" Bert paused in astonishment.

Austin smiled. "This is my fourth death, so I'm on Allocation Duty. What's it to be: guy or gal?"

"I beg your pardon?"

Austin tapped his nose and dropped his voice. "I went back as a woman in 1840. Spent a miserable life in domestic service. I tried to seduce my master to get a better deal, but I was so ugly I made Fungus the Bogeyman's wife look hot."

Bert stared.

"Or you could take a break from Life and return as a ghost."

"I thought ghosts were lost souls, stuck in limbo."

"Hollywood has a lot to answer for." Austin consulted his clipboard. "Hey now, how d'you fancy Hawaii? Make a nice change from the grey English weather, eh? I've got three babies being born in Honolulu in about ten minutes."

"This is so sudden."

"That's death for you, Bert."

"Hawaii, you say? I always wanted to surf."

"Now's your chance. Will I put you down for a male or female baby?"

Images of his wife screaming and snarling over monthly unmentionables, childbirth and the unfairness of womanhood flashed.

"Good god, not a woman. Oh no, no, no."

"Male then?" said Austin.

Bert rubbed his face, relishing the freedom from his hated mask.

"Uh, hang on, Austin. Do they have to cover their faces in Hawaii too?"

"The world over, Bert, the world over. They're saying an effective vaccine to eradicate the virus is still thirty or forty years away."

Bert looked at Austin. "I see. Maybe I could return as a ghost this time?"

"A ghost choice is a one off choice only and means you'll be earthbound for at least fifty years. You okay with that, Bert?"

Fifty years? Bert shrugged. With any luck, plenty of time for the virus to be confined to the history books. "Sounds fine to me, Austin."

"Good choice, Bert," said Austin with an unmasked grin.

The Air that I Breathe

Niles M Reddick

I found it somewhat ironic that Buddy's favourite song was *The Air that I Breathe* because in the last two days of his life on that respirator, he could barely breathe, and I suspect his breathing at work is how he caught the virus. Before I took him to the emergency room, he said between coughs, "Biden might win if he picks Warren as a running mate." I smiled and told him to hush, not to worry about that now, and that his health was more important than Trump or Biden. He hadn't liked my rhyme I'd made up and sang at supper last week, "Trumpty-Dumpty Sat on a Wall, a big wall, the biggest and best wall. Better than the one in China even. But even Trumpty Dumpty would have a great fall, the greatest of all."

Buddy vowed he would vote for Trump no matter what and we would cancel each other's vote. He didn't like Trump's spray tan and racoon eyes, the orange hair comb over, and his inability to speak in complete sentences, but Buddy felt Trump had done a good job, had fought harder than any underdog had, but I just couldn't stomach him, mostly for his unethical ways. I had previously thrown my vote to Hillary. She'd been a woman who'd suffered. God only knows what she'd gone through with Slick Willie, who I had also supported a long time ago, despite my commitment to morality.

The nurse came in with papers she had to complete because all data had to be reported locally and state-wide, but she wore plastic gloves and sported a fitted mask. Buddy, too, wore a mask that allowed him to suck in pure oxygen into his weakening lungs. She asked him where he'd been, but he really hadn't been anywhere, except the funeral home where he worked nights prepping bodies for burial. Buddy had shared his eccentric routine with her. He'd leave the house and take only right turns to the funeral home and back home. He never deviated. He was worse than Tesla had been in some ways. Buddy had prepped a lot of Corona victims and refused to refer to the rapidly spreading virus as COVID 19, but at least he'd dropped the Chinese word in front of it. He told the nurse he thought it was a new type of warfare, and he always wore gloves when dealing with the dead. He told her they weren't required to wear masks because no one was breathing, and the nurse asked him about the corpses exhaling trapped air when he was preparing them to be embalmed. Buddy told her he'd never seen that. He'd seen them pee and poop, and a limb move from a muscle contracting, but that was it. He struggled to remember the past couple of weeks, but he couldn't recall and fell asleep.

Buddy didn't last two days in intensive care, and I called the funeral home to let them know. The director told me he was sorry, that Buddy was one of the best employees he'd ever had and that the morgue would never be cleaner. He told me he would personally help me pick out the casket and plan the funeral, but I told him I didn't have the money and I'd have him cremated, that the hospital believed since I wasn't infected and he'd only been there, that it was likely he'd caught it from one of the corpses that had COVID 19 when they exhaled the virus into the room. The funeral home director said, "Oh, no. That's awful. Well, we'll take care of Buddy for you. No charge at all." I knew I had lit the fear of a lawsuit in him. If there was one thing I had learned from Buddy, it was how to get the best deal, and Buddy would be proud.

Sailing

Nicole Fitton

I want to have a tag on which to hang my feelings like a baptised disease. As if giving them a name makes them valid, allowable, acceptable.

"Yea, I've developed a bout of loneliness, the doctor reckons it'll take a few weeks to resolve, he's given me some pills, I'll be fine honestly, don't you worry about me."

If only life were that simple. But loneliness is a disease. It's taken away my soul, my confidence, my trust in my own judgement. I'm left with someone I don't understand, someone I don't want to be. I wait patiently until the house is sleeping, then spreading my wretchedness out like a blanket, silently, invisibly, I cry.

Some days are good. I make pancakes, plait the kid's hair. The world shines and I shine back. I talk to virtual people, me and the kids dance, and they smile, and I smile too both outside and in.

Lockdown came crashing into my world without a nod to my reality, my need for routine, for structure, and I bled deep and wide. I had not realised how taut, and thin, and long, so very long the tightrope had been. I watched as the smallest fragment of me slid away like mercury. My life is now the same swirling bucket as everyone else's except I've been swimming for months. On the surface my life probably doesn't seem that different; withdrawn, isolated, socially distanced at the best of times, functioning, but only just.

But I had been steering my lopsided boat. However badly I listed, I was still sailing forward. Now, the volume is too high and the control is broken. I am heading for the rocks and can already see despair holding a hand out to greet me. A collective of sleepless nights and fearful prayers move around me and I awake dizzy and slightly nauseous.

I turn on the TV and head straight for the news channels. I'm hooked on briefings, listening to the constant boom, boom, boom of the chatter is like an addiction. PPE, Nightingales, masks, will they mention the R number? Always listening for the chink, for the 'ta-da' moment when things will return to normal when I can return to my normal.

The kids are now at Mum's. The social worker took one look at me from the comfort of her upright dining room chair, and that was that. I stifle a laugh and am surprised to hear my voice out loud. It sounds gravelly and weirdly jolly.

I turn off the telly and take a look at myself in the mirror. If I squint, I can just about see it, the stillness of the water, the sails set perpendicular against the yards, unfurled and tied. I purse my lips together and blow. It's time to take back the boat.

I don my flowery face mask and find my keys. No one can see my gritted teeth, but my wild eyes show the level of my utter terror, I'm already at Defcon 3. Deep breathing, hyperventilation and a series of self-affirmations and by the time I reach the corner shop I'm reasonably OK. I'm surprised by the level of under population, although quite what I'd been expecting I can't say. I buy a packet of crisps, some Polos and a pint of milk.

Back home I wipe everything with antibacterial wipes and decide to have a shower (you can never be too careful). I phone Mum and smile when I hear the kids arguing in the background.

"I went out today Mum," I say as nonchalantly as I can.

"Well done, love, how do you feel? Danny put that down. Sorry love you still there?"

How do I feel?

"I feel OK," I say, and weirdly I do.

We chat about the kids, about the weather, about dad and his frustration at not being able to get the parts he needs to repair the lawnmower '*Bloody Covid',* and everything seems, well, it seems sort of normal!

It's six o'clock and for the first time in as long as I can remember I've missed the briefing. I flick the channels and find a documentary on Australian wildlife.

Tomorrow I will get the bus into town and see how far I can sail.

2020 Vision

C L Spillard

She stepped out to cross the wide, dusty road. No need to look – not nowadays. Empty roads and empty, cloudless sky.

A year ago – a year ago today – she'd picked her way through snarled-up traffic, battling with her umbrella against yet another day-long late spring squall. An hour early for a job interview, she'd ducked into the greasy spoon café in the Market under the concrete monstrosity of a car-park, to fortify herself with tea and a butty.

The Market would be closed now – closed because of the Virus. She leaned against the heavy, dusty glass door to peer in to the darkness.

The door gave.

A gush of warm air, laden with the whiff of steamy damp clothes, bacon and hot tea greeted her. The darkness buzzed with the hubbub of conversation; the low, hissing glissando of the hot water urn cut through it. She glanced about. The place was heaving! As if nothing had happened here since… well, for months. Who would come and risk it in this crowd? Perhaps all these people lived, like her, in confidence they'd already fought the virus off, and were immune. Or perhaps it was simply the least of their worries – relegated way below the recalcitrant toddler, the tight-lipped Gaffer and the ever-present rent.

She queued, chose her Full English, and having paid surveyed the busy café for a table—

Wait!

Wasn't that the bloke she'd talked with, a year ago today? The one to whom she'd laughed about her chances – *not had an actual interview in years, not for a proper techie job. Who on earth would take me, with white hair*? – still sitting there poring over his lap-top. Ethical Travel. Own business. Bet he'd run into trouble these days…

He glanced up from his figures, puzzled.

She looked a little tousled, but she was smiling. "Hello!"

"Er, hello again." Maybe he shouldn't ask. "Did you bail from that interview?"

"No! No – I got the job. But I'm not working at the moment: we're all on furlough."

He couldn't have heard that right.

"How's Ethical Travel?"

"Well, pretty much the same as earlier. We're making hay while the sun shines – in case the country goes mad and leaves the EU."

She was gaping – staring at him. Had he dropped something? Left his fly undone? She'd got up – was coming round, maybe to whisper so's to be discreet. But she pointed at the screen.

"I can't see the date on there. Can you just… click on it, so I can see?"

He did so. The screen showed: Monday 13th May. "My lucky day," he offered, with a sheepish grin.

"It's Wednesday. Your time-and-date's gone wrong."

"Nope: Monday. 13th May, twenty-nineteen."

She sat, like she was in shock.

She didn't touch her food.

"I… don't know about in here,"

He followed her gaze about the crowded, steamy Market, all views to the outside blocked by stalls hung with cheap merchandise.

"But out there it's belting-down sunshine, it's Wednesday, and it's twenty-twenty."

He said nothing. Maybe she'd make sense again in a minute. She'd seemed quite on-the-ball when they'd been talking earlier…

"And there's no traffic on the roads because we're all in Lockdown. So not much call for people like me, optimising traffic flow." She grinned. "So I'm on furlough. The government's paying."

She looked like reality had suddenly hit her.

"Listen: you said – did you – that you were self-employed?"

He nodded.

"So… well the government are paying people's salaries, but

only PAYE – so you'll not be covered. And nobody's travelling. Honestly – there are proper rules. There's not even a bus service, unless you're a nurse or something."

She indicated his screen once again.

"You might want a second line of business! Ethical Teleconferencing or something. Internet services, I don't know. There's no business travel anymore…"

He snapped the lap-top shut. "I'd better head. Sorry – I'm late for a meeting."

She picked up her fork and waved it at him as he beat a retreat. "You can say *that* again!"

She was laughing.

He breezed out of the door into white sunshine – dropped his laptop into slick Ortlieb panniers on his black Pashley Limited Edition.

He had everything prepared – connectivity for the Old Pump Rooms, his first job on a Grade II Listed building. He'd call them up from home, where it was quiet.

As he bent to slip the key into the D-lock he glanced across the empty, dusty road – a road both familiar and strange.

Beyond the bent steel railings opposite, the white-haired woman strode across the Square and out of sight.

Not My Children

Madeleine McDonald

Traffic came to a standstill when drivers abandoned their cars and vans, sensing the big moment was near. All across the world, crowds gathered in public spaces. In schools, hospitals, prisons and shopping malls, giant screens showed the same mesmerising image. The final two digits on the electronic counter clicked over faster than human eyes could register. Approximately once every 40 seconds, they read zero zero, indicating that the world had gained another hundred inhabitants. Viewers held their breath, waiting for the row of flickering blue numbers to show a nine followed by nine zeros.

Cheers erupted. Families embraced. Strangers high-fived. By the time the jubilant crowds had drunk their toasts and turned back to the screen, the blue digits on the counter had raced well beyond the symbolic number.

Alison and the dog took a longer walk than usual. Today, she had time. The school had arranged a special assembly for all the children to witness the latest milestone in the onward march of humanity. Nine billion humans.

Despite the pandemics and famines of the 20s and 30s, human ingenuity had risen to the challenge. New vaccines and new antibiotics had been developed. Food processing had improved, allowing nutrients to be extracted from the waste of yesteryear. Although disease and famine took their toll on the old, they produced only localised hiccups in population growth, for the predominantly young survivors were of breeding age.

Her small sons had already done school projects on the multiple challenges of feeding, housing and finding employment for Earth's increasing human population. Every technological advance was greeted by a surge of confidence and optimism.

Ever since her children were born, Alison had worried about

the future. Part of being a parent, she supposed. The world was changing too fast and there was nothing she or any parent could do. All she could do was keep her worries to herself and give them plenty of food and love.

One thing she had never anticipated was that parenthood would involve endless peace-making. It was not surprising there was always a war going on somewhere in the world, when her children found reasons to squabble every evening. They kicked each other under the table while drawing pictures of robots tending maize fields or rice paddies. Crops were thirsty and water was precious. From kindergarten onwards, every child was drilled in the importance of water conservation.

Today, relishing the break from routine, Alison followed the dog down a low-lying spit of land, thankful that animals made fewer demands than children. Patch ran ahead, periodically disappearing into a scraggly clump of grass, only his joyous tail alerting her to his location. To her left, waves scraped against sand and shingle. To her right, the incoming tide lapped at muddy river banks. Alison often walked the spit and always wondered why the sea had never breached it. She met only dog walkers, for the cows and sheep of her youth were now farmed indoors, in giant sheds. Pets were a luxury, and subject to a special tax, but people clung to the comfort they provided.

The river meandered through flat fields before running parallel to the sea for three miles, then emptying into a shallow cove scoured out by the tides. Beyond the cove, an outflow of murky river water fanned into the sea. On windy days, waves churned the incoming pollution into a froth of yellow bubbles.

When the boys were little, Alison and Patch used to walk with them in the double pushchair. As babies, they clapped their hands on seeing the bubbles. Now they pasted the slogan *More crop per drop* into their school books, not yet aware that massive doses of fertiliser leached chemicals into every watercourse.

At the end of the spit, where the shingle curved to form a tiny, rounded beach, Alison chose to sit on the grass rather than the pebbles, and allowed the breeze to caress her bare arms. She watched two gulls peck at something the tide had beached. Their activity attracted a screeching frenzy that vanished as suddenly as it started.

She lay down. Wriggling her shoulder blades and hipbones into a comfortable position, she was surprised to find the sandy soil under its thin covering of grass enfolding her like a foam mattress, adapting to her shape. Almost an embrace. She slid her fingertips through the surrounding grass, feeling tiny grains of sand between the rough stalks.

. Here, in her private place, she was alone. To her left a solitary container ship progressed along the horizon, sun glinting on its white-painted bridge. To her right, beyond the shallow cove, serried ranks of black solar panels glinted in the sunlight. Where clouds obscured the sun's rays, the panels became rows of leaden grey squares.

When the boys were babies, the fields had stretched green or golden. *Grey is the colour of non-life.*

No sound of machinery carried from the fields beyond the solar farm. Outdoor crops were now beets and cereals, foods that filled the belly but failed to satisfy the appetite. Luxury crops like fruit and vegetables were grown under vertical stacks of glass.

She feasted on solitude in greedy gulps, ears attuned to any interruptions. Once the population had passed the landmark figure of eight billion, privacy became a luxury. Beside her, Patch snored in counterpoint to the soothing crash of the waves. She pulled her sun hat down over her nose. Eyes closed, she relished the seclusion. Alison had no wish to celebrate the arrival of the nine billionth human alongside a brainwashed, eager horde of fellow citizens. *How will it end?*

She woke with a start but could see nothing. Cotton fabric lay warm across her eyes and forehead. What was the time? She tried to look at her watch but her head would not move.

Patch, where was Patch? She tried to call, but her tongue strained against the inert barrier of her teeth. *Patch,* she screamed. He did not come but she heard a grunting sound. *He's hurt. What's happening?* The waves struck the shingle in a monotonous rhythm; somewhere a gull screeched. The grunting came from her own throat.

With an effort of will, she stopped screaming and the grunting stopped. *My ears still work.* She listened but could hear no panting or barking.

Patch, her loyal companion for twelve years, would never abandon her. He must have gone to fetch help. Would anyone understand? The celebrations would be raucous, with feasts and firework displays. Would anyone notice a frantic dog?

She lay still and waited. Why did nobody come?

The air lost heat. The sound of the waves was louder, a relentless series of scraping shudders that reached her through soil, not air, as the tide slapped against slippery mounds of shingle. Underneath the vibrations, she detected another sound. A low, rumbling growl, like a dog warning strangers not to approach. The growl grew into a howl of rage, a wall of sound buffeted by the wind.

The children. They would find the house empty. Mobile reception was patchy here on the spit but she must try. Her arms would not move, could not move.

I'm coming, my loves. The effort to dislodge her sun hat cost her ferocious stabs of pain. She could see now where her feet had been, the trainers hidden under hummocks of soil and grass. Green tendrils bound her legs and torso. The pocket that held her mobile phone was sealed off. The primal fear in her gut told her Earth was reclaiming its dominion. At some level, she had always known, but had never imagined such speed and fury. *There is nothing we can do.*

In her mind's eye, she saw fragile, thread-like filaments piercing wood, brick and concrete. Ancient plants that humanity dismissed as weeds would carpet the roads faster than a man could run, making escape impossible. Across the globe, whether in darkness or in daylight, plants would engulf the jubilant crowds. Tethered and smothered, their bodies would rot, flesh and blood decaying into food for the tiny creatures of the soil. Earth, so long despoiled, would show no pity. Already vigorous vines held the boys' school doors shut and leaves heavy with sap obscured the classroom windows.

To her right, the river roared in spate, creating angry swirls where it met salt water. As the planet mobilised its deep resources, earthquakes released raging torrents to flatten mankind's arrogant citadels. Audacious towers of glass and concrete collapsed. So too the acres of glasshouses dedicated to hydroponic cultivation, allowing their meagre ration of water to escape. The waters of the globe roared seawards.

Earth vomited, ridding itself of parasites. Once the convulsions ceased, the water cycle would return to normal. Seawater would evaporate into rain. Animals would graze on ancient plants and their droppings would fertilise the soil in a cycle of growth and decay. As wildlife adapted and evolved, the soil had an eternity to absorb humanity's artefacts.

Alison lay unresisting in her green shroud, acknowledging her share of guilt in the plunder.

Take me. Not my children.

The plea went unheard, her grunts were dispersed by the vengeful howl of triumph that girdled the planet.

They did you no harm.

No harm except being born. The nine billionth person in the world, asleep in a cocoon of love, would also be culled, and the worthless carcass absorbed into the patient Earth.

Take me. Not my children.

The prayer was extinguished as paralysis reached her heart.

The New Normal

Clarissa Pattern

"Have you seen the news?"

My jaw clenches. Kam is fully aware I haven't seen the news. Which can mean only one thing.

"It's over," I say trying to keep my voice as neutral as possible.

Kam smiles their rarest smile, one that actually reaches their eyes and makes them seem to sparkle.

"Yep. Our all-caring, all-powerful, overlords have declared the world pandemic free. We can go outside again. We can meet other people. We don't even have to wear Hazmat gear anymore."

"I think it'd be best to keep wearing the masks. For a while at least. They've got it wrong before. Several times." I finger the zip on my jacket.

Kam laughs. "Why so coy, Nova? We've been trapped inside together for several eternities; we have no secrets. So just come out and say what you're thinking. You like my face being covered. You like our little protected bubble of two. You get off on the fact that you're the only one who gets to see how drop dead gorgeous I am."

"Poor choice of words," I mutter. "*Drop dead* when so many have died."

A raised eyebrow. "As if you care." Kam flounces off to the bedroom.

Probably to try on and select an appropriate post-pandemic outfit to declare they're back in the world and as glorious as ever.

But still I am grateful. For the time we've had together while the world has been in isolated mourning.

But still I am grateful that when Kam called me out for still wanting to wear masks, they focused on my protectiveness of their attractiveness. And not the insecurity of my own unattractiveness.

A tremor goes through me at facing the world unmasked. Will things be like they were before? How did I cope before? I can no longer remember. But the deep pain of all those side glances, the jeering of the teenagers, the coldness of the adults, the false empathy of people pretending to be kind… all that and more… is too unforgettable. How will I cope with everything being back to *normal*?

"Apparently there's going to be a new normal."

Ignoring the crumpled sheets, and an unfortunate spilt tea stain, and crumbs from this morning's breakfast/lunch/afternoon snack-in-bed, Kam lies on their front, their feet are continually crossing and uncrossing. They swipe quickly through one internet article after another.

Half an hour ago Kam threw a black sack in my direction. I've only just summoned the energy… courage… will… some other positive quality that other people have in abundance… to start packing. I slowly move around the room, taking as long as possible to select the few items that are mine and mine alone. I'm hoping that I can get away with leaving my toothbrush, sensitive toothpaste, towel, and pyjamas. Which doesn't leave much else to take. I've been wearing Kam's clothes, reading Kam's books, using Kam's soap, and what else is there that a person really needs in their life?

"The new normal appears to be exactly the same as the old normal," Kam says as if I've asked for an explanation. "Just with less of us. And maybe with fewer cars. Maybe with fewer planes."

"That's good then? Give our planet a better chance of surviving? Less pollution. Stop the polar bears drowning in melted ice?"

I'm not that aware of what I'm saying. I keep picking up and putting down the expensive scent I've found hidden in a dusty corner of Kam's dressing table under miscellanies that include: two love letters from a name that Kam has never mentioned; rubber bands in a variety of colours; a chain of paper clips; underwear that neither of us has ever worn, nor would ever wear; and a fluff of hair pulled out and discarded when cleaning a brush. I bought the scent for Kam long before lockdown, the costliest gift I'd ever dared to give them, to commemorate the decade that had passed since we first met. Would it seem churlish to take it? Or worse, would Kam encourage me and tell me to give it to someone else who'd actually appreciate receiving a pricey present from me? Most probable, and worst of all, Kam wouldn't notice, even though I'm standing right in front of them as I make this momentously insignificant decision.

Kam is talking about… world things… when I put the scent back and replace the mess back on top of it.

"I guess I should be going," I interrupt Kam's spiel.

Kam stops speaking and looks directly at me and then at the almost empty black sack.

"That's all?"

"That's all."

I drag the sack behind me as I walk to the front door. Kam remains on the bed.

I try not to think of Kam. I try not to think of the tiny bedsit the cured world is forcing me to return to.

How many days is it since I've been *home*? How many days is it since I've been outside?

Kam and I took a walk in the rain the first time the restrictions started to lighten, peering at the world from behind our masks, holding hands as if that was what we always did. But then when death rates spiked again, I remained inside no matter how the rules yo-yoed back and forth. Kam, as always, has been more flexible, taking deliveries of our rationed goods, and sanitising up to venture out and explore the barely-stocked shops on the occasions they were allowed to be open.

When I creak the door open, brightness surges in, though the sky looks all grey clouds. As my eyes adjust it becomes clear everything is the same as it ever was. Road, pavements, cars, walkers, a couple of discarded beer cans rattling in the breeze, but that is all. Post-apocalyptic destruction, or ghost town emptiness, would somehow be less disappointing than the mundanity of a pandemic leaving no visible scars on the street where Kam lives.

Something taps me on the shoulder. I jump before my brain can reassure me it's Kam. They've come to say goodbye to me after all. I melt myself against their form in a full body caress.

I can't restrain myself from saying, "I'll miss you."

"Don't."

"It's not something I have a choice about. It's how I feel," I say.

"No, I mean, don't miss me. Stay with me. Even though you don't need to, even though we could go out now and meet other people, stay with me."

I straighten myself and gaze into their eyes waiting for the joke or sarcasm to hit me.

"Nova. Think. Why did I ask you to stay with me during this whole long lockdown thing?"

I shrug. "Because I was convenient, comfortable, easy for you when other hook ups were risky."

Kam's mouth twists to the side. They sigh. They pinch their nose. "Okay. Yes, that is all true. But in a screwed-up world, convenient, comfortable and easy has a lot going for it." They turn and pad away from me. "You're letting too much cold air in. Close the door and come to bed with me."

I want to pause, to think. In less than a heartbeat I obey and follow. The post-pandemic world can wait forever. Kam can't.

Number 45

Robin Wrigley

Robert struggled through the last row of barbed wire stopping momentarily to unhook a barb from the leg of his corduroys and started to wade through the grass on the racecourse marvelling at its height. At the far side he ducked underneath the barrier and looked to his left to ensure he was alone before he turned right along the path towards the grandstand.

As he progressed, memories of happy days he had spent along this very path with thousands of other horse racing enthusiasts came flashing back. Like so many simple pleasures gone or declared illegal he endeavoured to blot them from his mind. There was no point in perpetually mentally anguishing about the million things that had been missing from his life, things that he had no power to do the slightest thing about. Life, such as it is, is what it is, and he had to get on with it or end it. Something in his darkest moments he had contemplated.

Just before he reached the corner of the grandstand he jumped back, his heart thumping putting his hand to his mouth to smother a cry of alarm as a fox flashed in front of him and disappeared through the long grass of the course. Animals had no sense of social distancing he mused to himself, forcing a wry grin in an effort to raise his spirits. He didn't want to meet Vic with a miserable face.

At the corner of the grandstand he stopped and checked all around to ensure he wasn't being observed when he was startled yet again by a shrill whistle. He looked up and saw his old school friend waving at him from the top row of seats.

He calmed himself and waved back and started to ascend the steps up the side of the seating until he reached the last row. He walked along; hand extended in a handshake before the pair hugged in a thoroughly heartfelt manner totally ignoring all the rules imposed on them in the last number of years.

"Bobby! So how the hell are you? You old sod." Vic's smile reached from ear to ear across his weather-beaten face, the face of a man who had spent his life battling the elements. Despite his advancing years, well into his eighties, he still looked in good shape apart from the slight stoop he had developed.

"Oh, you know much as I would like to complain, not too bad Vic. Leastways unless I break our longstanding agreement not to mention our ills and failings. I'm fine thanks. What about you? Any news of the kids? Are they managing to survive long enough to let you have a day off to come down here?"

"They're all fine thank God and Graham's marriage has taken a turn for the good as he and Georgie have come to their senses and decided they had to stay together if only for the sake of the kids. I think she would have left him some time ago. I wouldn't have blamed her. I think she realised just how bad it is out there, at least during this never-ending state of affairs. James and his brood are thankfully still in the outback of Oz and seem to be doing okay. Of course, they are lucky with the size of the place and that they are not governed by quite such a bunch of self-serving numbskulls like we have been blessed with."

"Talking of which," Robert chimed in, "I know and this prick Starmer is not proving to be any better, is he? I thought when that silly girl knocked Boris off of his bike it was divine intervention. Just goes to show it really doesn't matter who's in charge when Mother Nature and the bloody Chinese are against you."

"She got ten years for that you know."

"The *Mirror* thought she ought to be awarded the Victoria Cross." Robert continued but personally thought the George Cross would have sufficed. "I mean it wasn't proved she did it on purpose."

"Come, come mate let's not be doing politics this early in the morning and ruin our day. Have you brought the goods?" Vic replied holding out a crystal tumbler in earnest anticipation spreading over his face.

Robert unzipped his Barbour wax coat and fished out a bottle of Scotch whisky from his poacher's pocket along with a crystal tumbler from the other pocket.

"You don't really think I would forget, do you?" he joked passing the bottle to his friend.

"Only eight years old, you tight bugger." Vic scrutinised the label.

"Never mind that. Just get that cork out and let's have something to help us forget for a while. I've thought about nothing else on my walk this morning. Took me nigh on an hour today, you know. There was a time not that long ago I could do it in half that. Course I wouldn't have to walk at all if those crazy bastards in Extinction Rebellion hadn't demolished Fawley."

Vic poured them both generous measures of whisky, pushed the stopper back in the bottle and placed it on the bench between them. He rested his glass with it and took a jar of pickled walnuts from his jacket pocket unscrewed the lid and placed it next to the bottle.

He picked up his glass again and raised it in the gesture of a toast to his friend and the pair drank from their glasses.

"Phew that tasted bloody good even if I do say so myself"" Robert exclaimed with the smile of a satisfied man.

"Hold on a bit there, Bobby, you only carried the bloody bottle. I think our friends north of the border had a little bit to do with this, didn't they?"

"Fuck the Jocks. Don't get me started on that subject Victor."

"No, I won't. Here try one of these walnuts; Georgie pickled them from our own tree last year."

"How is the farm in general?"

"Suffice it to say it could be better," Vic replied offering Robert another splash of whisky. "However, I was pleased the other day when Graham actually asked for my opinion about the planting of next year's crops. That was the first time for that in a while. What about you? Still rumbling around in number forty-five on your own?"

"I am but I guess when I go, I will be the last member of the family to live there. Elizabeth shows no sign of wanting the place. To be honest Vic we don't get along well anymore. She is more French than English now and we don't see eye to eye on anything.

Reckons I am a combination of a dinosaur and a hayseed. I can't forgive her for not coming home for Eleanor's funeral last year. She said Michele claimed it was too risky for her and her darling boys to travel. I was devastated, but there you are. And, of course the book of French heroes is a pretty thin volume." Robert smiled in an attempt to make light of a subject that was in fact still troubling him.

"Sorry to hear that Bobby. What about the neighbours? Any more of them snuffed it or moved out?"

"As you know the couple in number thirty-nine moved into a care home. Old Sandra next door passed on a couple of days ago. I suppose I will be obliged to go to her funeral, though I don't know why. We were never that close, and I don't think I would know her kids anymore. They didn't visit that often even when her old man was alive."

"Old George you mean? He was a decent sort wasn't he from what I remember?"

"Yes, you've got a good memory Vic. You're right he was a really nice guy, not that I saw much of him in his last years. Sandra put a stop to that. Reckoned I was a bad influence on her husband. She wasn't the first wife to think that now I think of yours when she was alive."

"Hah, Anne always thought you were a bad bastard as you well know. But, hey let's not dwell too much on the dead and the past. There's bugger all we can do about it. Here, have another scotch. It's not bad despite its age you know."

"D'you remember that day old Jim Randall backed that outsider in a three-horse race and it romped home?"

"I most certainly do. The memories of the night after are a bit dim though." The two old friends guffawed in unison sipping their drinks.

As the wintry sun moved out from behind a cloud and cast long shadows over the desolate racecourse, they leaned back against the wall of the grandstand and lapsed into silence grateful of the friendship that had survived all these years.

...And Then, One Month Later...

Ray Suchow

Barely a month ago, our families were torn by the brutal reality that we couldn't gather in person to honour the first anniversary of your passing. The difficult but absolutely necessity of social distancing measures required by the rapid spread of the virus wouldn't allow it. Although there was the small mercy of being able to meet online, remember, and comfort each other for a while, it wasn't the same... could not have been the same... as being with family in person – especially since I wanted to hug your two young sons, my nephews, who now grow up without a father. You were son, brother, and husband; truly the flame that burned twice as bright but only half as long... and then the hell of Covid19 hit us all again.

In what twisted nightmare reality does watching your younger (and only) brother die, as you watch helplessly by his side, count as a positive? Welcome to the era and aftermath of Covid19. For not one month later, the majority of our family was denied even that privilege as our mother began to succumb to the ravages of three different illnesses... while being alone for weeks except for her nurses, a few quick texts while she had the strength, and nightly news of the virus' continuing rampage which could not have been any comfort at all.

Mother had always been strong – a fighter in so many ways. And so, even as she fought the latest flare-up of a respiratory illness, and then shingles as it set in, we were confident that in time she'd recuperate, be released, and we'd have her amongst us once again. As her agony continued, her husband was finally allowed to see her, and he visited every day so we had the comfort of his updates and she had the comfort of some real company at last. All would be well in time.

On a bright Saturday morning in early May came the phone call informing us that she was no longer wanting to take food. The nurse was quite alarmed. In her present condition, she would only have a few days at best. She also told me that she'd add me to the list of allowed visitors as soon as she could, clearly breaking protocol and risking her career. The logic of being extra cautious in case I infected my mother with something else became completely moot; there was literally nothing else I could bring that would worsen her condition.

But still I held hope that the fighter I knew was still there, and would respond to a good, affirmative chat and so begin her recovery. Thus I arrived on the Tuesday – the first day I could be put onto the daily visitors list – as a messenger from the family, ready to lovingly but firmly tell her to 'smarten up and get better now because we love you and we miss you!' That resolve vanished the second I saw her.

In that searing second, I went from a messenger to being a son at the bedside of his dying mother.

As I took her hand she winced with pain; even that contact was too much for her. We spoke briefly. She told me to tell her husband to pay his credit card bill; clearly her mental faculties were still intact. This strongly reinforced the rationality and finality of her decision. We spoke of her pain, that even after a lifetime of being an indomitable spirit – of learning how to walk again after polio as a young child, among many other triumphs – the pain was finally too great. She thanked me for being in her life; I thanked her for giving me mine. She smiled, though it pained her. And I asked if she needed me to be her advocate to the family, and she gratefully agreed. All too soon it was time to give her a gentle kiss on her forehead – somehow she had the strength to lift her head up – and I left with tears in my eyes yet a pride in my heart that I could carry out her final wishes.

They were her final words, for she passed the next evening.

As I look back on that day and compare it to my brother's swift passing – brought back to vivid life barely a month ago – I do have the comfort of sharing her last words, of being her advocate to the family, of being with her in her final lucid moments. I'm also eternally grateful for the blessed mercy of that nurse, who bent bureaucracy so a mother could see her only surviving son one last time.

Yet these comforts were denied to the rest of my family. And, due to Covid19, how many countless other families have struggled with similar situations? How many have been denied even the mercy of a few last moments with their loved one? Tens of thousands at least, with thousands more to come.

The individual stories of Covid19 continue to unfold in a brutal blend of forced separations and tragic deaths, but also of resplendent examples of humanity. In the midst of this hell, and in its aftermath, hope still shines. For that, I gaze heavenward and humbly give thanks. This fragile hope still sustains me as the virus continues to spread, and as our valiant healthcare workers (and so many others) continue to fight it. When this is all, finally, over and done with, and I can gather with what's left of my family and honour together, I'll dearly remember those who have passed. I will also give Blessed Thanks for that angel of a nurse who risked all, so I could have a few final moments with my mother whom I loved beyond all words.

Loco Lonnie

Susan A Eames

Rumour and speculation cloaked the old man like a mystery. He sat at a table in the jangling bar, elbows akimbo, guarding his personal space. A stranger brushed against him and then careened away in shock when the oldster snarled and made to bite.

Some said he had been a scientist, complicit in spreading the virus. Others said he was the epidemiologist responsible for finding the vaccine. Whatever the truth of it, something had happened to the old Englishman to make him flee to this remote Spanish town. The locals shunned him because of his anti-social behaviour. They called him Loco Lonnie.

Lonnie finished eating and pushed his plate aside. Between gulps of acidic wine, he worried at strings of lamb lodged between his teeth.

A group of labourers spilled in. The cacophony in the bar rose several notches. The old man scowled and rose from his table. Stiff-limbed, he scuffed across to the bar counter through a chaos of discarded peanut shells, olive stones and empty sugar packets.

Ana rattled through the beaded curtain from the kitchen. Bony collarbones poked above the neckline of a dress that should have been cut up for rags. She smelt of garlic and wore the look of a woman resigned to a joyless life.

Lonnie pushed some coins towards her. Without making eye contact, Ana nodded and lifted a carrier bag onto the counter. Her right breast jiggled from the effort. Lonnie stared as the breast settled into immobility, drooping slightly lower than its sister. He slid his tongue over his teeth.

The oldster picked up the bag and left the bar to cycle back in the spring sunshine to the place he now called home.

He eased himself off the bike and propped it against his Well, hawking and spitting in one fluid movement. Two straggly dogs jostled him, snuffling at the carrier bag.

"Get off me."

He spared a glance at the vegetable garden and chicken run. The chickens were reproducing well and many of the vegetables were close to harvest. A harvest which should see him through the winter and allow him to keep his town visits to a minimum.

He entered his farmhouse, ducking as a piece of plaster fell from the lintel. In the kitchen he rummaged through the bag of raw offal which Ana thought she had given him for the dogs. He picked out specific organs and laid them to one side.

Outside, the dogs were fidgeting, toenails tap-dancing on the tiled porch, tongues lolling, tails wild.

"Alright boys, I'm moving as fast as I can."

He tipped the remaining contents of the bag into bowls encrusted with food debris. There was a scramble of fur and bared teeth.

"Oi, oi! Steady."

The dogs settled into their meal. The old man sat and leant against the wall of the house. A Hoopoe called *poop poop poop*, drowning the soft cluckings from the chickens. A persimmon fell with a splat. He wrinkled his nose at the sharp tang of over-ripe fruit. The dogs swapped places to check each other's bowls. Lonnie's face creaked into a smile.

Like miniature lions stalking their prey, a feral cat with her half-grown kittens approached, the smell of the food overwhelming their disdain for human contact. When Lonnie saw the cats his smile vanished. Growling, he picked up several stones and threw them violently at the animals.

"Bloody vermin. Go on, get lost."

A stone ricocheted off one of the kittens. It yowled and stumbled in its dash for safety.

"Hah, got you."

The dogs fought the distraction, heads bobbing up and down, torn between the desire to chase the cats and the compelling need to eat.

The oldster's face softened. "It's all right lads, finish your dinner. The thieving devils have gone."

Wriggling his shoulders against the warm stone as if he were trying to burrow into the wall, he settled himself. A gecko skittered away, looking for smaller prey. The dogs lay down, sated. Lonnie looked towards the chicken run again with a frown, but all was quiescent. He relaxed and closed his eyes, somnolent in the balmy air, thinking about the old days when he worked in a strange land.

There was plenty of time before he needed to go down to the cellar to monitor his latest experiment.

The Immuners

Susan A Eames

The island didn't show on the charts. Tilting coconut palms rimmed the beach. Clumps of wild ginger in scarlet and magenta grew in abandon under the palms. Rainforest clad mountains rose inland. Ray and Amanda anchored Bella II and rowed ashore in their little dinghy. They pulled the dinghy clear of the high water mark and stood listening.

After nearly three years at sea not only were the couple tired of their diet of fish but also their stock of dry goods and vitamin supplements was perilously low. They had been able to keep the yacht's rainwater tank topped up in these rainy, tropical waters but they had agreed that it was time to risk landfall in search of fresh food supplies. But only if they could do so in safety. Their discovery of this unknown island was a godsend.

"I don't hear anything but birds," said Amanda with a smile. She took a few steps, fighting the wobbles as she transitioned from compensating her body to the movement of the ocean to moving on dry land again.

"No, it's tranquil enough, isn't it?" said Ray. He pulled a machete out of his rucksack and began to hack at the ginger fronds. When he'd cut a decent amount they piled it over the dinghy to camouflage it from casual glance.

After checking the hidden dinghy from all angles Ray said, "It'll do." He looped the rucksack onto his back. "Come on. Let's see what we can find."

They headed inland. Within minutes they found remnants of a track discernible in the undergrowth and halted in alarm.

"Humans?" Amanda said.

"Animals more likely. Look how the disturbance only occurs low down. All the growth at head height is undamaged. I think it's fine and hopefully it means there's fresh meat to be had."

They ducked and wove along the rough trail which twisted and turned through the trees. Sunlit mountains sluiced with pencil thin waterfalls towered. A sharp bend and the path collided with a tannin coloured river running beneath a tableau of pyramid shaped peaks. It was perfect.

They shadowed the meandering river through a wide gorge and came upon a grassy sward flanked by casava plants. Delighted by their find, Ray used the machete to loosen the earth and dig out the tubers. While he was digging, Amanda explored the immediate area and spotted papaya trees. Many of the fruits were still green but she knew that green papaya was edible and would store well. Their foraging was going well.

She knocked down a couple of ripe papayas and walked back to where Ray was working.

"Refreshment time."

She took the machete from him and deftly sliced the fruit.

They sat by the river to eat in silence, almost reverently savouring the sweet, tangy smell. Their first taste of fresh fruit in years.

Amanda licked her lips and went to rinse the juice from her hands. She spoke over her shoulder as she squatted by the river. "This island was a good choice for our first landfall. Maybe we should think about staying here?"

"Hmm. We'll have to see, love."

Amanda stood. "I'm tired of running, Ray. Tired of being afraid."

"We haven't even established if the island is uninhabited, Mandy. And Bella is vulnerable while she's anchored out there. We'd have to find a way to beach her safely and then hide her. That wouldn't be easy, you know. She's too heavy to just drag up the beach like the dinghy. We'd have to rig a pulley system and cut down trees to make poles to roll her. We can't jeopardise our only means of escape if there are any marauders still out there."

"Well, I know it wouldn't be easy, but it could be done. Let's at least consider it. Please? We could make a start tomorrow at reconnoitring and mapping the island." She looked up at the mountains. "Those mountains might run down to the water on the other side of the island and there might be caves large enough to hide Bella."

"Of course we'll do some exploring and consider the possibilities, love."

She threw her arms out in enthusiasm before sitting down next to Ray again. "To think we might actually have found a refuge. We could stop running, at last. Could stop wondering when we're going to get caught either by the marauders or by the authorities." Amanda shuddered. "Could stop imagining what they'd do to us if they discovered that we're Immuners. To finally stop worrying about the horrors of either being turned into lab rats, or being tortured, raped and killed by the marauders." Amanda paused before adding, "I'm tired of being on constant alert, Ray."

"I know, Mandy. I know." Ray precisely placed the papaya skin on top of his discarded seeds, aware of his wife's fears and his need to protect her. "But we've been safe at sea, haven't we?"

"For how much longer? We can't live on Bella permanently. This island is remote enough. It's uncharted, so no one even knows it's here. It's like Conan Doyle's Lost World." Amanda took hold of Ray's hands. "There's something so calm and soothing about this place. I just know we won't have to worry about any dangerous surprises here. I feel it in my bones. And we've already seen that it can sustain us. If we decide to live here maybe we can seriously think about our future." She touched her abdomen. The gesture was tentative but specific. "Ray, you do realise we could be the last healthy people on earth? The last people capable of building an immune colony. A new start for the human race."

Ray stared at Amanda, startled.

"Sorry, that sounded a bit pompous, didn't it?" she said.

Ray grinned. "Well it might have sounded better if you'd said we could be the *first* healthy people in this *new* world instead of the last healthy people from the old one. And, umm…" He fussed with the papaya rind. "We'd need to find few more Immuners like us to make a colony genetically viable."

Amanda chuckled. "You old romantic, you."

They exchanged goofy grins.

A scalp-raising screech reverberated through the mountain range.

"What was that?" said Amanda.

They looked up at the pterodactyl flapping straight towards them.

Ray and Amanda blinked.

The 12th Crusade – A Story of Our Time

Henry Lewi

In the year of our Lord 2024, Pope Urban IX and The Holy Roman Emperor King Arthur VII of England called for a Western Crusade against China. The 'Terrible Chinese Sickness' had swept the Americas and Western World four times with the loss of almost a third of the population during that time. The economies of the affected countries lay shattered and there was growing anger directed at the Chinese Empire where the sickness had begun its journey across the world. The disease had been brought to Europe by ships and merchants travelling from the Far East to Europe, first landing in the big ports of Genoa, Marseille and London. The Church had first declared the plague a punishment from God because of the pursuit of science and pleasure by the people of Europe. In 2020 the church banned all science within the Holy Empire and forbad its use by physicians in treating people affected by the plague; and ordered that all Universities pursuing science be closed, and shut all medical schools not associated with the church.

Belief in the church became paramount and every wave of plague was greeted with the litany "God Wills It."

The Holy Roman Emperor, a direct descendant of King Arthur of England (the eldest son of Henry Tudor) and his wife Queen Catherine of Aragon, together with their cousin the son of Louis XXII of France were to lead the forces of Europe, those of the Spanish and French Empires and their colonies in the Americas, eastward to the far edges of the dark continent of Asia. At the Emperor's behest the Vatican lifted the 500year-old ban on muskets that had been ordained in the 7th Lateran Council of 1641. Commanding the massed forces were the Bishop of Mainz Freidrich Hans Guderian, the notorious Russian Cleric Metropolitan Grigory Zhukov and the French General Maximilian Bonaparte whose grandfather had conquered India for the French Empire.

As the crusading armies coming from all parts of Europe and

their colonies began to congregate in Western Russia, the Pope blessed the Emperors, Kings and Commanders of the various armies in St. Peter's Square as they presented their Standards in preparation for the Crusade. Amongst the banners raised, were the Royal Standards of England and Spain, the Oriflame of France, the Eagles of Germany, Russia and Poland, and the Black Cross of the Grand Master of the Teutonic Order.

So, like a vast wave, the two million strong 12th Crusader Army of Europe steadily moved across the vast plains of Russia and Kazakhstan towards China, like their predecessors had done before them. The army travelled not by foot or horse but by steam train and steam driven motorized vehicles packed with men armed with the newest form of musket, crossbow and artillery pieces; with the aim of laying waste to Wuhan and then onward to Peking. It would take months to move the army to the Chinese border where the enemy waited.

As the crusading army moved ever eastward, reports reached them of a Chinese army that had developed sinister weapons of destruction and a new form of transport that was translated as an 'Infernal Combustion Engine' powered by a substance called Oyle. Weapons were said to be far more advanced than those of the crusading army, with one being called a 'rapid gun' capable of discharging hundreds of pieces of shot or 'bulets' within a minute. There were reports that the Chinese army had an evil machine called an 'Armoured Fighting Vehicle' that carried a huge gun and armour to protect its men, and worse, being powered by Oyle it could travel extremely fast. Despite this King Arthur would gather his commanders and urged the armies ever onwards repeating the mantra of the church and Crusader "God Wills It"; and so the Crusader army of Europe moved eastward to meet the Chinese army in the battle of Lake Balkash in Eastern Kazakhstan. There was no crusader miracle as there had been at Malta, Lepanto and Turkey, the battle was one sided and within 7 days the Crusader Army of Europe was annihilated and the Chinese Empire moved Westward conquering all before them, completing what the 'Terrible Chinese Sickness' had begun in the early days of 2020.

Aftermath 4/10/2020

Maeve Murphy

I have to say if Lockdown was almost like a relaxing break, to spend quality time at home growing vegetables and writing and creating closer bonds with family, this second spike that has started is harder. I think we all thought somehow it would all be magically over by the summer and everything would be fine. But it isn't and now there is talk of it not being over until next Easter.

For someone who is involved in film today, Cineworld announcing a closure of all cinemas in UK, Ireland and USA is sad, demoralising and one hell of spirit crusher. And yes I got across to see my mum in Belfast in August, but when will I get to see her again? My nieces back in school have had their first covid test, and the result was negative, just came in today. And I have enjoyed the quality time with my husband, but Jesus, 24x7! And what about my friends! And what about Christmas?!

This second spike is harder, for me. If there was ever a time to pull out your strongest inner spirit for yourself and others, it is now. Yep it's time to bring the inner Rocky out and start metaphorically running down the street with the kids and up those steps, every morning. Maybe not quite at 5 am. But if needs be! To survive this, I need to be even stronger and find purpose in it and bring people along with me when they start to dip. And people are feeling it.

So yes I have re watched Rocky 1 and 2 and have the rest to get through. And yes this is a female film maker talking about male boxing films. But really as we know, it's not about the boxing; it's about the fighting spirit. It's about winning.

So while one film project has for now stalled, I seem to have got new shoots for another one, by none other than hard graft. So I guess I am adopting a gratitude for what I have. A desire not to just think about me and me and me, but to keep supporting others, and to show somehow in my own way, and in a way that is particular to me, that this time, was positively life changing. Somehow the making of me.

So I am getting ready for my Rocky run, in my heart, in my spirit, tomorrow morning.

See you on the steps. Victory by Christmas!

Lost and Found

Tony Domaille

I never dreamed it would turn out like it did. Now it's all over, I find it hard to remember exactly what I was thinking, but I know I didn't take it seriously.

You see, I'm pretty thick skinned. When they said we could only go out for essential reasons, or an hour of exercise, I ignored them. I saw the neighbour's curtains twitching every time I walked out my garden gate, or jumped into the car, but I didn't care. If people wanted to press pause on their lives, that was up to them. If they wanted to believe the doomsday merchants, and let daytime TV fill their dull little lives, it was their lookout. Even when I got stopped by the youngest policeman you've ever seen I didn't feel the slightest anxiety or regret. I lied to him that I was on a mercy mission to my dying mum, with essential medication. He waved me off with sympathetic words. No deterrent.

I was mightily ticked off that they closed the pubs, but my like-minded mates and I quickly found a way round that. We bought boxes of beer from the supermarkets and took it in turns to make our front room a bar. Dart boards went up on the walls, Alexa became a juke box and we got to play cards for money without some snowflake publican worrying about his licence. It was going alright, considering the government had tried to imprison the whole population, but then things began to change.

Nick was first to crack.

"I'm giving the meeting up a rest," he said on the phone.

I laughed. "Tina got you under the thumb?"

"No," he said. "It's her mum. She's got Covid."

I said, "Well that's a bummer, but you haven't been seeing her, have you? You can't have got it."

He said they hadn't been seeing her, but she'd got ill in her care home and three old dears had died there. He said it didn't feel right breaking the rules when people were dying. Looking back, I regret calling him a sheep. I should have been more sympathetic, but it annoyed me he was changing things for me.

Then it was Mark. It was his turn to run a bar but, when I got there, he wouldn't let me in. He reckoned he'd seen some scientists on telly with the Prime Minister and they were all saying it was dangerous and wrong to break their rules.

I said, "You still owe me eight quid from cards."

"I ain't got it," he said. "They're letting Shelly go from the takeaway and we're running short. But soon as I'm flush again…"

And then they dropped like flies. The blokes I thought were my mates all turned, one by one, into snowflakes, afraid of a germ and afraid of getting caught breaking the rules. Suddenly I was drinking cans by myself in my front room and breaking out the Scotch to relieve the boredom. I guess it's no surprise that Carol didn't like it.

"You're drinking too much," she said, and the conversation always went the same way.

"What else is there to do?"

"What does the rest of the world do?" she said. "Couch to 5K. Tidy up the garden. Do that decorating you never get round to."

I laughed at her. "If you think I'm going to find work to do when, for the first time in my life, people are paying me not to work, you're nuts."

She pointed out that my furlough money was down on what we were used to. She told me that we were getting behind with our bills and what I was spending on drinking would be better covering the electricity. Then we argued, the arguments got worse, and I started sleeping in the spare room. If I wasn't having the government telling me how to live my life, I certainly wasn't taking it from my wife.

It's surprisingly easy to find the part of the world that isn't locked down, and I found it. If my mates and my wife weren't going to give me a life, I was going to get it elsewhere. So, I found a couple of little illegal drinking dens downtown. And though I'd always said any bloke who paid for sex was a loser, I decided these were exceptional times.

I picked up the first girl… no, that's wrong; the first girl picked me up at the makeshift bar. She asked me to buy her a drink and then she asked me if I was looking for 'company' just like they ask in the movies. She whispered a pricelist in my ear and the deal was done out the back.

You'll say it was inevitable I woke one day with a cough. All the contact I had with so many strangers. No social distancing, masks, or hand gel. Carol told me I couldn't go out and that I had to isolate. Even then I would have ignored her if not for the fact I felt so rough. Going out wasn't on the cards.

At first, I thought I was ahead. I'd had months of living as I pleased, and a touch of flu-like illness didn't seem like a particularly expensive price to pay. But then it took a turn. It started getting harder to take a breath. My temperature soared and I couldn't smell or taste anything, even if I'd felt like eating. When the ambulance came, it felt like I was watching someone else being loaded onto a stretcher with an oxygen mask over my face.

Carol couldn't visit me in hospital. She had to isolate but, whilst she had symptoms, she didn't get hit as hard as me. I started missing her, but I couldn't take phone calls because I couldn't get my breath to speak.

When they moved me to ICU, I knew it was getting really bad. I hadn't ignored all the news and I knew that some people went in and never came out. That's when the fear started to really take hold. That's when the regrets started to kick in.

I always thought that when we died, that was it. Now I know that's not true. I can see you. You just can't see me. When the pandemic ended, and people went on to live a new normal, I was left behind. When I died, my number was added to the tens of thousands who lost their lives to the virus.

I watch Carol sometimes. People are good to her and listen sympathetically when she talks about my death. But it's hard hearing her tell them that I'm no longer here because I couldn't find a life in restriction. That I couldn't find the joy in what was closest to me.

So, in the aftermath of the pandemic, I find I've learned what really matters, but I learned too late. Is it too late for you?

In a Bubble

Brigita Orel

I've always liked going to book festivals and not just for work. But I've also thought that people you meet there are often pretentious. As though they're something more, something better because they're enlightened – along with a glass of wine they also intake literature and culture in general. Perhaps they thought the same about me. But perhaps they didn't even notice me.

The two women in front of me are certainly paying no attention to anyone around them. They're deep in conversation, rushing to tell each other everything that's on their minds before the talk with the famous illustrator begins. They grumble about the pandemic measures, including the ones which require the seats in the hall to be spread out and no food or drinks to be offered at the venue. They keep repeating, indignant, how it all affected their lives and work so terribly much.

I'm just happy that the strict lockdown is over. This is my first event since March. I couldn't wait to get out of the flat. I was hoping Aaron would come with me but he was afraid he'd be bored and cranky. I don't like going out on my own, but the smell of freedom after being quarantined for so long was just too sweet to pass up this opportunity.

Few people are indifferent to the changes in our lives these days. I was lucky. As a literary critic, I wasn't affected that hard. I'm used to working from home, with the only difference being that I had to share my office with Aaron. Often during the two months, I took refuge in the living room or on our small balcony to avoid listening to his video calls with his co-worker Martha. Maybe people in marketing are more talkative by nature or maybe it's a requirement of their job but they were so loud. Her laughter would resonate from the office almost daily, her jokes and anecdotes from her lockdown life were something I'd gladly have avoided. Every time I passed Aaron's desk, I would see her fix her thick long hair with a gesture that was too big for the laptop screen. She tilted her head just so. I felt sorry for her. She seemed such an attention seeker. The anti-covid measures must be torture for people like her – no meetings, no kissing, no hugging. When you're an extrovert and flirtation is your second nature, how do you function if you're not allowed to meet and mingle?

The hair of the woman sitting in front of me is almost the same shade of brown as the co-worker's, but her hair is tied into a neat chignon. Her hands gesticulate as she talks so her blood-red nails reflect the overhead lights in short, startling bursts.

"You don't understand," she says to the black-haired woman next to her, "how very boring his wife is. So dull. I've seen her a few times. There's nothing remarkable about her. Nothing that would attract a man like him."

I'm not surprised that their conversation started with complaints about the strict measures. That's the new normal these days. But they switched topics faster than most and went straight to gossiping.

The black-haired woman now says with a conciliatory tone, "Many relationships are in trouble because of the lockdown. It's easy when you see your partner just for an hour or two every day, sometimes less. The lockdown changed that."

"True. But he's been planning on leaving her even before all this. Long before."

"Why hasn't he, then?"

The brunette waves her hand dismissively and her bracelets jingle. "You know what men are like. Shilly-shallying and trying to figure out what will pay off and what won't. He's afraid she'd wring him out. She doesn't work much, I don't think. It's mostly his money."

"That sounds so mercenary. I'd expect a marriage, even when it's over, to be about more important things." The black-haired woman shakes her head.

I can't but agree with her. I can't imagine being more concerned about money or property or a car than about Aaron. Everything comes second to someone you love. If I had to choose between money and Aaron it's clear what – who – I'd pick. Maybe that's because we've only been married for a few years. Maybe I'll be less of an idealist after twenty, thirty years, but I wouldn't count on it. A sincere relationship is important to me, the depth of emotion, honesty, devotion. Our relationship was being tested during the two months of the lockdown, of course. Aaron was sometimes abrupt and impatient with me and I was stressed and worried that I won't have any more work because publishing houses postponed or stopped new publications. But when the weekend started, we relaxed on the couch with a glass of wine and chatted and laughed.

It's funny, though, how the current atmosphere of panic affects us all. We seem to be more apprehensive of every touch. Even lovers, I think, behave more cautiously. There's less cuddling and more hand-washing. I wish all this would go away. I miss Aaron and how comfortable we used to be, how he caressed me and kissed me. We had a crazy good time together. I can't wait to get all that back once this is over.

The words of the dark-haired woman pull me back to the present. "Two of my friends are divorcing," she says. I can't hear her next words because she takes off her jacket and makes a lot of noise putting it away. "It makes you think, doesn't it, how we can't live in close proximity with our own partners for a few weeks. Says a lot about our relationships."

The brunette leans closer to her and drops her voice but I still hear most of what she says. "In his case, the lockdown may have been the last straw but he's been thinking about it for a while. Plus…"

"Yes?"

I almost lean forward. Now I'm interested in what's going on, what the big reveal will be.

For a moment no one speaks and then the black-haired woman's face – what I can see of it from the side – clears and she blurts, "Oh!" And then in a forced whisper, "You two are having an affair?"

The brunette lifts her hand and I imagine she presses her finger to her lips to silence her friend. She gives a small nod and her friend giggles, but the high-pitched sound is more disbelief than approval.

"It's more than an affair," the brunette says. "We're real. Solid. It's a good thing the lockdown's over. Those two months, I thought I'd go crazy when I couldn't see him. I kept imagining him spending time at home, every night sharing his bed with his wife. It's nearly killed me."

"I can imagine. All this 'living in a bubble' is pretty tough for most people."

"He managed to slip away once to meet up. Do you have any idea how uncomfortable sex in the car is when you're in a rush? God."

Her friend giggles again.

I wonder why such people come to book festivals. I don't see these two enjoying a good book. Maybe a bodice ripper but not Hilary Mantel. Not that I don't enjoy both. I read a romance last week and I'm not ashamed to admit it. I needed a bit of comfort in these strange times. Aaron's been distant lately. He isn't as used to working from home as I am and it stresses him out. I don't want to push him to make love to me. Things will fall back into place now that he'll go back to the office.

"I regret that a bit," the brunette admits then. "It's almost spoiled everything. But at least he was in a better mood afterwards."

My stomach turns. How awful to talk rubbish about a woman just because she's got to a man first. So much for visitors to book festivals being better human beings. So much for morality and mutual respect. I can't imagine the pain of this woman, that wretched feeling of betrayal and rejection. How can women do this to each other? Why? How many women betray their best friends this way? As if one person's emotions are more important than someone else's. I'm not surprised we don't know how to live with each other any longer when we have no empathy, no understanding, no selflessness. Sometimes I'm appalled at the world we live in. The world we create with our behaviour.

The black-haired woman now sits facing her friend. Four

necklaces dangle around her neck and her eyebrows are too accented. Otherwise, her face is attractive and kind-looking. "What excuse did he give his wife?"

"That he's going to Jewson's or something."

I almost smile at that. Shops like Jewson's were probably visited most often apart from grocery shops. Everyone was after gardening tools and building materials. Aaron went to B&Q several times. Twice, I went with him. The last time, just before the lockdown was lifted, he went on his own because he needed the space in the car for the wall shelf which he then never installed. When I was in the cellar last time, I forgot to look for it. Perhaps I should give it a try installing it on my own. He was adamant he buy it. He yelled at me – actually yelled – when I wanted to go with him, saying there wouldn't be enough space in the car. I attributed his brusqueness to him being fed up with having to stay at home but it still hurt.

"He bought a wall shelf for my living room. Aaron's wife thought he was buying it for their apartment," the brunette says.

Her laugher is interrupted by a cry. When the two women turn to stare at me, I realise it was me crying out and that the brunette is Martha. The loud, coquettish Martha. My husband's co-worker. Her laugh fades away now, blood drains off her face. Her shell-shocked expression looks comical on her self-possessed face. Her friend reaches with her hand into the space between us as though to stop a non-existent scuffle.

"Martha?" I blurt. "What?" It seems impossible. "What are you talking about?" They can't be talking about my Aaron. About me. What's this all about? He isn't leaving me. They're wrong. There must be another Aaron who bought a wall shelf. And who met up with his lover. With Martha.

It makes no sense. We've only been married for five years. We're comfortable with each other. He said, only months ago, that we should think about having a baby. A baby. I was so happy. I've dreamed of having a baby with him almost from the start. Does he want to have children with Martha now?

He told her that I'm dull. He's never said that to me. But during the lockdown he talked with her more than he did with me. I remember her giggling and laughing and him laughing with her. He barely ever laughed with me during the two months. He hasn't touched me. When I went to kiss him before I left earlier, he turned his cheek, not his lips. How could he do this? How?

There were no signs. Nothing out of the ordinary. Except maybe that he wasn't quite so loving as at the beginning of our relationship. But that's normal. It happens to every couple. Doesn't it? Why didn't he say something? How didn't I see this coming?

"How dare you?" I say to Martha but the words are a howl of pain. I'm shaking with the need to say something hurtful to her, to scream at her. At her friend, for being shallow and mean. At Aaron for betraying me. But I can't form words. A keening sound escapes my lips. I must look pitiable: the unremarkable, bespectacled woman upstaged by the flirt with curves. I hear my heartbeat in my ears and I don't comprehend the words of the host as they resound through the hall. And then everything in me crumbles and the sights and sounds rush at me.

"Poor girl," a woman nearby says.

The microphone screeches and then loud words fill the hall, followed by an applause.

People start to avert their faces, they've lost interest in the little drama unfolding now that the host and the illustrator have come on stage. But I keep staring, frozen to my spot, when Martha blurts, "You'd find out sooner or later…" Her friend is tugging at her arm. My view of her blurs. I wipe my clammy hands into my sleeves and then see they're wet from tears. Martha gives a shrill laugh and turns away. My body is overcome by tremors, my chest contracts in a sob.

The chair makes a hair-raising sound as I push it back. I can't breathe in here, I must get out. I don't know where, not home, but away from here. Anywhere.

I try to put on my mask but it tangles in my glasses and earrings. Another humiliation. I hold it on with my hands as I stumble towards the door. The mask at least hides me from all these people who've witnessed my shame. I feel their pity coming at me in waves. They know nothing about living in a bubble. Or of the horror once it bursts. Nothing at all.

Red Mist

Susan A Eames

"You here again?" The old lady folded her arms.

"Hello, Mary." Gillian put her briefcase on the occasional table.

"Come to pester me just when they bring me… bring me… oh, what's the blessed word?" Mary thumped the arm of her chair. "Dinner. That's it. Me dinner."

"Sorry, Mary. It's been a busy morning and I'm running a bit late. But I thought you wouldn't mind me joining you while you eat."

"What have they given me? Smells like steak and kidley. Lift that lid off, Lovey. I loves steak and kidley. Never could make it like me Mam though."

"You're looking well, Mary. How are you settling in?"

"I forget where I am sometimes. 'Specially when I wake up in the morning. I lie in bed with a sick, sickled… sickly feeling in the pit of me stomach."

"I'm sorry to hear that."

"Why do they call it a pit?"

"I don't know."

"Mine isn't like a pit. More like a hill. Sticks up even when I'm lying down. Hand us me tea, Lovey."

"You look more relaxed than you were on my last visit, Mary. And you've brushed your hair. That's good to see. Can we talk while you eat perhaps?"

"Talk? You always want to talk. Ooh, this *is* steak and kidley. Good."

"It's because I'm here to help you, Mary, and I can't help you if we don't talk. We have to understand what happened, don't we?"

"Do we?"

"Yes. Do you remember where we finished last time?"

"No."

“We talked about impulsive behaviour, didn’t we? And we talked about the consequences of impulsive behaviour.”

“You like your big words, don’t you?”

“Do you remember our chat?”

“I don’t know why I have to keep… keep… what’s the word? Repeating. Repeating the same thing. I already told you. I already told them. Where’s the sugar?”

“Here you are. I’m sorry if it makes you uncomfortable, Mary. But you have to talk to me about it, otherwise I can’t help you.”

“Didn’t see it coming, did I? Always did ignore the blessed obvious. But this one’s a biggie, isn’t it, Lovey?”

“It is.”

“So obvious with… hindsight. Yes. Hindsight’s a powerful curse.”

“Were you happily married, Mary?”

“What sort of question is that?”

“Were you?”

“Don’t talk soft.”

“Is that a No, then? Why didn’t you leave him?”

“Love, was it?”

“You tell me, Mary.”

“No, don’t ask me. Love, hate, what does it matter? It was my lot, wasn’t it? Look at that. Why have they given me these little green… whatchamacallums?”

“Peas?”

“I don’t care for peas. Told them before. I *like* the steak and kidley though. Never could cook a good steak and kidley like me Mam. Never got the hang of suet.”

“Why do you say it was your lot?”

“What?”

“You said you thought it was your lot, Mary: to stay with your husband.”

“Well that’s because it *was*, Lovey. What else could I do? Ordinary folk didn’t separate. Didn’t get… what’s the word? Divorced. Not in those days. Dirty word wasn’t it? Not like the film stars. You made your bed and you had to lie in it. You took what life throwed at you and you couldn't complain. We all took our chances with our marriages and we accepted our lot for better or worse, didn't we?"

"And you didn't have children."

"Wasn't to be."

"Did you want children, Mary?"

"Don't talk soft. Who doesn't want children?"

"Did you blame yourself for not being able to have them?"

"Well, who else would I blame?"

"Him? How do you know it wasn't your husband who was infertile?"

"Daft talk. It's women who bear the children, not men. Didn't he always tell me that? This is lovely gravy. I could pick up the plate and just lick it up, I could."

"He hit you sometimes, didn't he?"

"But then I'd spill the blessed peas. Horrid little beggars."

"Mary?"

"We used to lick our plates when we were kiddies: me and my sisters. But only when Mam wasn't looking. Our Mam would thump us good and proper if she caught us. Always telling us to mind our manners she was."

"Mary? Did your husband hit you a lot?"

"I already told you, I don't want to talk about that anymore."

"Did he blame you? For not giving him children? Is that why he used to hit you?"

"Gracious, listen to her."

"Mary, did he refuse to share the responsibility with you? Was that it? You said he was always telling you it was women who bore the children. And wasn't it him who made you see a doctor about it?"

"Didn't do any good. Still makes me blush: what that doctor did to me. Called it a Medical Examination. Medical Examination, my eye!"

"But your husband didn't get himself examined, did he?"

"You're not married are you, Lovey?"

"Why do you say that?"

"If you was married, you'd know the rules."

"Tell me the rules, Mary."

"A husband has… what was that big word you said?"

"Responsibility?"

"Yes, responsibility. A husband has a… responsibility… for bringing home the bacon and a wife has a… responsibility… to give him a family and keep a tidy home. Here, give us me pudding."

"So you couldn't leave him?"

"Sponge, is it? Sponge and custard. Lovely!"

"Mary? Is that why you couldn't leave him?"

"That's it."

"Or, is it really that you *wouldn't* leave him?"

"Couldn't? Wouldn't? What difference does it make?"

"It might be important, Mary."

"Listen. He was a clever man and I was stupid. Didn't he tell me enough times? I was so stupid and useless I couldn't even give him any kiddies. He used to say he didn't know why he put up with me sometimes. And, I was stupid: too stupid to even think about leaving him."

"He manipulated you?"

"Like to sound clever, don't you, with your big words?"

"But you had a choice, Mary."

"Choice? What choice? Where would I go? Back to me Mam and Daddy? Or one of me sisters with their own husbands and kiddies? You think one of them would have taken me in? That they wouldn't have minded about my shame? No, Lovey, not on your Nellie. Women had to accept their lot. That's it."

"But, Mary…"

"I couldn't let myself believe I had choices. Not when I was too… sick… sickled… sickly stomach churning scared. There, I've said it."

"I see. You didn't think you had a choice because you were scared of him? Is that right?"

"Scared. I just told you, didn't I? I kept hoping. Hoping something would happen to him. When that virus flu thing started my life got much worse. You know?"

"Covid?"

"The doctor kept telling us to be careful because we were vun… vun…"

"Vulnerable?"

"That's it. The doctor and the people on the telly kept telling us to stay indoors. Drove me barmy. Stuck at home with him and nowhere to run. Of course I was scared. He had me proper trapped. Turned me black and blue whenever he felt like it. Sometimes I had new bruises on top of old ones. Oh, how I wished he'd catch that Covid thing. Or me. I didn't care. And all the warnings gave me hope. They kept telling us we could catch it if we weren't careful, so I *wasn't* careful. Didn't hardly ever wash me hands. Kept waiting and hoping. But then… poof! They found a cure. No more danger. No more people dying from it. Dashed my hopes proper that did. There I was, still trapped and still scared of him. As usual."

"So, what changed, Mary? What happened to your fear?"

"My fear? I… I don't know."

"Mary? It's OK. Take your time. Why did you do it?"

"Because… because…"

"Yes?"

"Where's me tea?"

"It's here. Don't change the subject, Mary. You're nearly there. Tell me why you did it?"

"Oh, Lovey. I hoped he'd catch that Covid thing and give me peace at last. But it wasn't to be. I was disappointed. No, not disappointed. I was angry. Angry with those people who found the cure. Boiling over angry with them for dashing my hopes. Is that why I did it? I don't rightly know. All I know is that when I was carving the meat that day and he thumped me, it wasn't just his walking stick that broke."

"What do you mean, Mary? What else broke?"

"Red… Mist. I heard someone call it that. Over sixty years married before I saw that Red Mist. And it was our dinner time. I was carving the meat. Wasn't that his bad luck, Lovey?"

"Yes."

"Didn't I give him… what's the word? Surprise."

"You surely did."

"Turns out I didn't need that Covid thing to get rid of him after all."

"No."

"Will they keep me here, d'you think?"

Jack the Lad

Dawn Knox

Jack. Jack the Lad, his friends called him.

Covid-19? Who cared? According to Jack, the world was full of viruses and no one stayed home in case they got a dose of 'flu. Of course, if you were old or sick you'd have to look out for yourself.

But what did Jack care? He was young and healthy. He looked after himself, working out in the gym. He played rugby. He was tough.

Let people fend for themselves, he thought. He only mixed with people of his own age and if he walked past someone in the street who was vulnerable – well perhaps they shouldn't have been there anyway?

When he first experienced dryness in his throat and an irritating cough, he ignored it. A cold had never held him up before it certainly wasn't going to slow him down now. He continued with his day-to-day activities and if he strayed into somebody's personal zone of two metres, well did it matter that much? The government guidelines indicated he should self-isolate but they had also urged people to 'Eat Out to Help Out'. He preferred the latter advice. If the government couldn't decide on a clear policy, he'd do as he liked. And anyway, didn't alcohol kill viruses? A few pints would put him right.

He couldn't remember the following week; it had been a blurry nightmare populated by masked and gowned people; by tubes and bleeps and something clamped over his face. But he'd survived and after a period of rest he knew he'd be as good as new.

Everyone had overreacted. Yes, okay he'd been told he'd had a bad dose of Covid-19. But he'd come through and with some exercise he'd be as good as new.

But he wasn't. And years later, he realised he'd never achieved his earlier standard of fitness. 'Long Covid', they'd told him. It was nonsense, of course, just a fancy name. Anyway, he could live without a sense of smell. And if his lung capacity was much reduced, he blamed his age; after all, no one remained young forever.

But Jack was wrong. Some people did remain young forever – at least they stayed young in other people's memories. Those who died young were forever in the minds of their loved ones, their faces still as they were many years before, unmarked by the lines and creases they would have accumulated had they lived. Those for example like the barmaid Jack had flirted with in his local pub who'd died shortly after he'd been taken ill with Covid-19. And two of those who'd nursed him during his stay in hospital had succumbed to the virus, and had later died.

But he'd been all right.

Jack the Lad.

Jack the Mad.

Jack the Bad.

But too arrogant and unprincipled to ever be Jack the Sad.

The Best Things in Life Are Free (or Are They?)

Lynn Clement

Mike Dingwall closed down document, *CVD 2019*, but not before he'd re-encrypted it. He sent it to the darkest recesses of his electronic memory-bank. He knew it would be years before anyone got to see it. He'd had it classified for another quarter of a century. In 2069, he'd be dead anyway, so what would he care.

His genius idea for making billions would remain his secret.

There was a knock on his door. Dingwall passed his hand over a button and the hermetic seal to his pristine office swooshed open and re-sealed itself behind the visitor.

"Sir, there's a problem with Pod-Section 4273," said a muffled voice, through a mask.

"And…" said Dingwall.

"Sir, some pod-dwellers are not paying their bills."

"Because?" said Dingwall.

"Sir, their branch of the electrolysis station has been closed down. They can't work so they can't pay."

"And that's my problem, why?" Mike Dingwall didn't get to be the richest man on the planet by being nice. In fact, he got there by being evil.

"Send in the Carters," he barked.

The Carters arrived at Pod-Section 4273 with a screech and a belch of hydrogen sulphide from the cart's exhaust. Behind their individual screens, the pod-dwellers held their collective breath.

All checked they'd paid their bill by tapping the gauge on their kitchen walls.

Lyall Monk's gauge beeped. There was a bang on his door and he knew it was the end.

The cart was parked outside his pod. Two Carters in red and yellow striped Hazmat suits stood by his screen.

He'd been laid off from Dingwall's Electrolysis Plant for four months now and hadn't paid his oxygen bill.

The electric lights crackled and the beep on the gauge grew louder. Lyall began gasping for air.

His neighbours watched as his body was thrown onto the disposal cart. The Carters marked Llyal's pod-door with a red X.

The neighbours all checked their gauges again.

Mike Dingwall, CEO of *Oxygenius*, the world's only supplier of breathable-mix oxygen, picked up the photograph of him shaking hands with President X.

He smiled, drawing his thin red lips over his pointed canines.

The photograph was dated December 2019. Twenty-five years ago. The date they'd released CVD19 upon the unsuspecting world.

Mrs Hunt's Guest House

Susan A Eames

Mine was one of the few guest houses that survived the pandemic. In the aftermath, I positively flourished in this new, altered, world.

The old school style of guests was gone. No more foreigners on cultural visits to experience an English Seaside Town. In this new world, foreign travel was now an anathema. And no more pensioners! In this new world, the elderly had been erased.

I embraced the new breed of survivors by welcoming them and tolerating their little foibles.

'Live and let live' became my mantra. After all, I felt lucky to be alive.

Before long, I almost forgot the old days and the new norm became, well, normal.

But when Jodie started howling at the moon my world altered again.

A deep growl had woken me: a dissonance that sort of stretched until it elongated into a full blown howl. I blinked. Why was the sound reverberating *inside* the house?

At breakfast no one mentioned the nocturnal howling. Mr Canid pick, pick, picked at his food, as per usual.

"Eggs aren't to your liking, Mr C?" I said.

"No, they're delicious."

But he didn't finish them, as per usual.

Jodie changed her order. "Just bacon and sausage please, Mrs Hunt."

"No eggs? No toast?" I said.

"No, thanks," she said.

The howling woke me again, filling the empty spaces in the house. I investigated. It took but a moment to establish the howls were coming from Jodie's room. My mantra might be, 'live and let live', but this really wouldn't do.

After breakfast I took her aside. "I can't have you disturbing the other guests."

Jodie bared her teeth.

That night I went to close the curtains against the bothersome glare of the full moon. Jodie and Mr Canid were loping across the lawn. They stopped and stared straight at me.

When I joined them they nodded in satisfaction and we threw back our heads to howl in the moonlight.

The New Hope

Henri Lewi

I have to leave, life here is too restrictive." The thought kept repeatedly coming into his mind. "But how and where?"

The pandemic had not recurred or returned as it had never gone away. Time and again the European countries had gone into lockdown but always the virus recurred. After 6 years there was still no effective vaccine but as always there were rumours that one was imminent. Europe now resembled its pre-Second World War map of isolated separate countries with closed borders. The EU had failed in its first major test and all hopes of a great and powerful 'United European State' had all but disappeared. The United Kingdom had fragmented into a number of individual countries with restricted entry and little freedom of movement between them. Public transport had disappeared because of the lack of staff and the fear of travelling on the buses, trains or the various underground system, and the health service existed only to provide an emergency service or care to those infected by the virus.

In the six years of the pandemic the British government had had six prime ministers just like Henry VIII wives: Resigned, Died, Collapsed, Resigned, Died, and Survived. But the government was very different. Now a government of national unity, there was no opposition and certainly no debate when the 'Threat to Health and Life Bill' was passed. This law gave the government complete control over all aspects of public and private life, effectively ending all public gatherings whether for sporting events, protest meetings or simply allowing the public or private meeting of more than six people. The police and the army were now effectively combined into a Civil Defence Force and were able to carry out detention and isolation of individuals through their 'Track and Trace' powers. British society had manifestly changed, with over 80 per cent of the adult population on some form of government benefit or 'furlough' payroll with the government controlling food, fuel and medication availability. Restaurants, shops and pubs remained closed during the repetitive lockdowns and fewer and fewer were reopening as restrictions were repeatedly applied, relaxed and applied yet again and again.

Now the European Governments were announcing a mass vaccination program with a new anti-viral vaccine based on nanotechnology, which, if you followed the numerous conspiracy theories would further enhance monitoring and restrictions on personal behaviour and freedoms.

He was lucky; he had survived the Virus in its earliest first round and was one of the few lucky ones to develop antibodies and had seemingly remained immune throughout the last few years. Additionally, he had donated his antibody rich plasma on a number of occasions, but after the third outbreak the local hospital had stopped asking, and despite repeated calls they had seemed uninterested, and had not got back to him. On the positive side he'd been issued with a Biometric European BioPass because of his immunity. The Pass recognised throughout Europe (with the exception of Russia and Belarus) contained his immunity data, fingerprint and retinal prints, as well as facial recognition so could only be used by him and him alone. There were numerous reports of isolated self-sustaining or 'free communities' being set up all over Europe. They were free of government control, but with no access to banking, medical or Wi-Fi services, so trying to find them would be problematic. He knew of a number of 'free communities' in West Wales and the Scottish Highlands and presumed there would be quite a few in the poorly populated but much less restrictive Scandinavian countries. Interestingly, whilst Denmark had stringent border controls between its southern European neighbour and at its maritime borders, the border between it and Sweden only existed during the phases of lockdown, but once restrictions were relaxed there was little effective border control between the two countries; especially across the Oresund Bridge, which was the road link between Denmark and Sweden across the Oresund Strait.

Over the last couple of years, he had progressively purchased small bars of gold, platinum and palladium as well as a plentiful supply of gold sovereigns, Kruggerands, salt, sugar pepper, and 100 litres of diesel in 20 litre Jerry cans. He still had his old shotgun and two boxes of cartridges, though with his licence nearing expiry, he knew if he didn't move it he'd soon have to give the gun up; and he still had his two bows from his old archery days though only a dozen arrows, which were now becoming increasingly unavailable. He'd taken the time and trouble to research the best cold weather tent, (the AO10 Arctic Oven Tent) for the cold Scandinavian winter weather, which he'd directly purchased from its Alaskan supplier. As the various lock downs had eased, and temporary European travel had become possible, he had gradually ferried various items over to the lock-up garage he'd rented in Fredericiagade 27 (in Copenhagen), just back from the port area on the island of Zealand. Also stored in the lock-up was the black 4-year-old Toyota Landcruiser he'd bought in Holland and driven directly to his Copenhagen garage; it was in good condition, less than 35K on the clock and yes only 'one careful owner!' The beauty of the lock-up was that it was no distance from the E20 whereby he could easily access the Oresund Bridge, which put the sparsely populated regions of Sweden, Norway and Finland within easy reach. A 12 hour drive could take him as far north as Trondheim in Norway or Ostersund in Sweden, but a shorter five to six hour drive (just at the limit of a full tank in the Landcruiser) would take him to Varmland County and Karlstad with access to the huge area occupied by Lake Vanern, where the virus had had minimal impact.

So, as the lockdown was again eased in Europe in early April 2026, he packed up his car, (an old Mercedes E class) and from his home in a little village in Essex, drove via the Channel Tunnel (which had remained open throughout the pandemic) to Copenhagen, essentially following the A1 and bypassing the cities of Antwerp, Dortmund and Hamburg. He was allowed to pass through the many restrictive motorway and border controls by virtue of his passport and BioPass, and he knew his data and journey was being logged on the various State data bases. The journey to Copenhagen took him over 20 hours and he had arrived at the lock-up in the early hours of the morning. He transferred what he'd transported with his Mercedes and loaded up the Landcruiser and settled down for a quick sleep. Six hours later fully refreshed, he took the Landcruiser picked up the E20 and crossed into Sweden via the Oresund Bridge. As lockdown in Europe had now been eased, his Biopass allowed him to cross into Sweden. From the bridge crossing he picked up the E6 driving northwards to Gothenburg, bypassing Helsingborg and outside of Gothenburg he picked up Route 46 and headed into the sparsely populated area of central Sweden onwards toward Skara. He skirted the old and very small city and continued onward towards Gotene and finally somewhere outside the town he turned off the main route and headed into the unpopulated woodlands bordering the southern coast of Lake Vanern.

He had effectively left the now very restrictive British society behind, and was now alone and his own master. He could take his time seeking out these 'free communities' as they were calling themselves, who were not above or beyond the law, but just living a freer life well away from the stifling controls of the various European Governments.

Maybe just maybe he could sit out the pandemic, or at least until it became totally controllable, either here or within a 'free community' and he could maybe sometime soon return home to a relaxed and much less restrictive and normal Britain, he truly, truly hoped so.

Conversion

Sally Angell

Shannon is a single parent in her twenties. We see her in her house, after Lockdown is lifted. She is wearing jeggings, and a patterned top, her hair scraped back, showing big hoop earrings.

When the Volkswagen Golf pulled up outside this morning (*looks out of side window*) I couldn't believe it. It had to be her, Ms Fancypants from the Little Unicorns Nursery – or Pre-school as she calls it. They get more money if it sounds educational. I thought, *What's she doing here? Slumming it.*

Well, I panicked, and snapped at Gabby to get her shoes on. She hasn't worn any for weeks, and I'd forgotten the effort it takes, trying to squash her feet into them, doing the straps up. We've just been getting up when we feel like it, eating Ready Brek two o'clockish, in our socks if we could find any. Gabby's been bored and hyper with the nursery reopening delayed, wanting to see the other kids, but now she looked like she was going to make a right scene about going back.

"Hi Shannon." Emilia, that's the nursery woman's name, said on the doorstep. They usually call me Mrs Foster as I'm one of their mummies. "I thought you might like a lift." She'd obviously been able to get a hair appointment, perfect style and colour. Mine's still all shaggy and horrible. "I hope you didn't mind us leaving the provisions the other week. We just wondered if you were all right. Being on your own." I wasn't answering the door back then even if I was dressed, so I didn't see the food box until later when me and Gabby went round the estate for Our Daily Exercise.

"Oh yes, thanks," I said.

Emilia was peering into the hall. Could she see the tools in the kitchen? Don't want to go back to it, but what else can I do? I pulled back, so used to trying to imagine a six foot person lying on the floor, between me and someone else.

And I thought, *She knows.*

Fades out

Shannon is sitting at a low table, wearing a plastic apron.

When we got here, to the nursery, I said, “I can stay if you like.” Nothing to eat at home except chips and sausage for tea tonight. They’ve got a coffee machine here, so free drinks and biccies all day, and when the kids have lunch there’s sandwiches and fancy snacks for the adults.

On the way here, she, Emilia, said she’d got to call in home for hand sanitizer; she’d forgotten it. We don’t have to use it now, but she said can’t be too careful. I sat there in the car on the pebble-dashed driveway, telling Gabby not to scuff the seats, in shock ’cause I hadn’t realized where we were. I pictured the tiled hallway, that day last year, the bin bag with a label stuck on it. *For Oxfam.* I hadn’t been able to resist a peek. Posh clothes. Looked new. Not as if it was stuff she wanted.

Back in the car, Emilia was going on about her husband being furloughed, perhaps he’d have to get another job. She turned her head. Lily’s mum said you work at night. Right, I thought, that’s the nosy woman from the flats. I said, “It’s evenings. My neighbour minds Gabby.” Well, it’s not a lie. The teenager next door babysits because I let her bring her boyfriend in.

“What is it you do?” Emilia said, all chatty. I was looking out the car window. I don’t usually bother with the Newbuilds now. I prefer the big old houses, in the classy area, which we were passing now. Mostly elderly people live there. They have routines, so you know when they’re in.

“House Clearance.”

“Right,” Emilia said.

“I only go round to see what’s suitable, make lists,” I explained.

"Inventories," she said. "How interesting."

That's one word for it, I thought. They cut my Universal Credit a few months ago because the Garden Centre wanted to increase my hours. So I left there, had to find something else.

Any–way, here we are in the Art Corner, doing painting. Well potato-printing. I'd like to have been a teacher, if my school hadn't been so crap, and me not being there most of the time. I want Gabby to be different, not like me.

To be fair, this is a good nursery. They take the kiddies on the free childcare, as well as those who pay. I like it here. When I was at home Staying Safe in lockdown, my neighbour did actually get us some food on her Tesco delivery and I had enough money to pay for it because of not going out. And also there was a rent holiday. So I could just play games and do fun things with Gabby. I remember thinking, *Is this what other parents, other moms, feel like all the time?*

Shannon is back at home

Emilia was stacking chairs at home time, when she says, "Do you want a lift home?" I said, No you're all right. We'll walk.

She looked at me, and said, "Can I have a word?" I thought, This is it then. She does know. What will she do? I'm for it. And what's going to happen to Gabby?

Shannon stares out of the window.

Emilia swung a chair onto the top of the pile. "As you see, Shannon, we're short-staffed."

I said, "Yes, where's that girl with the glasses? She's usually here."

"She got it," Emilia said. "The virus."

"Oh no."

"She – died."

Well that threw me. Couldn't have been more than twenty. Emilia was saying something. "We wondered, would you like the job? You're so good with the little ones. It would be proper regular hours. And training, when we can sort that out. It might take a while, how the government is at the moment." She said it was OK if I had to work notice on my other job.

It seemed too good to be true. Was this a trick? Would I really fit in there? But people are making changes in their lives now, doing something different. This could be a whole new start.

I said, I'll think about it. I can come in tomorrow anyway. I took my apron off, and called to Gabby. As we turned to go Emilia stared at me.

"I had a top just like that," she said.

Note about this story

The idea for this story came from something I heard on the radio:

> *Some occupations are difficult to continue in Lockdown. Burglars are out of work at the moment!!*

MASK

Angela Elizabeth Armstrong

Up lit,
Back lit
In a secure case of glittering tempered glass
Whose reasonable dimensions belies the captured display
And whose magical prisms distort the reality
Of the power and symbolism of the object within.

On a black velveted plinth this anti icon, this emblem of sorrow
Rests amongst a scene of mud and crispy faux autumn leaves
Distorted, shrivelled, crumpled in shape akin to the bed on which it displays itself…
An artist's impression of a time we once knew.

Its sight speeds the mind back to another time
Its function an obligation by deed and by need.
This barrier method, this disposable, 3 in a packet guardian of the pleated variety…
detested, despised and cast off when opportunity warranted
On pathways and pavements, a portent mingling with the usual detritus and discarded by
Dirty humans at their finest and selfish to the core.

"Who would ever have thought it…"
An acknowledgement,
A muted utterance, unfinished yet understood completely
From fellow onlooker glancing the oddly beautified symbol
Whose glance is knowing like mine and all those who were there.

I linger no more at this aide-mémoire of human catastrophe
Aware of its oppressive story seeping into my soul and catching me off guard
I walk.
A deliberate manoeuvre to escape the oppression

I aim for vault like doors and walk through
And close them tightly shut.
A deliberate act
Acutely aware of my action to keep the terror within
And away from daylight and sacred life.

A dismissive toss of my entry ticket let go from clenched palm and placed in a bin
And rid myself of its declarations
'25 Anti Iconic Symbols from the first 25 Years of the 21st Century: Time and Place'
A Small Donation is Welcome on Entry. All proceeds will be passed to local charities
Enjoy Your Visit to Middleford Museum
… My skin tainted with its red ink, from being grasped too long, noted from a peripheral glance
A prompt, a distant flash of a need to cleanse for fear of a poisonous touch.

I move on
I sit on a park bench
And breathe in the sweet summer breeze to refresh my spirit and lungs
I feel the sun on my back and it warms me within.
I ponder and reflect
And feel grateful and blessed for the life I have.
In no time at all, a fleeting moment,
I am visited by a Robin who flies past my eyes
And settles amongst brambles to sing its song with conviction
This lovely manifestation encourages me to lift my eyes to the sky
And I smile back at the day, knowing all will be well.

Aliens

Jim Bates

Abr and Bnr were two aliens sent to earth on a fact-finding mission from the planet Zerros by the supreme commander, Knx.

"Find out if the planet is ripe for take over," Knx told them. Collecting planets was a hobby of his, and he was in the mood to add to his collection.

"Will do," Abr said.

"You can count on us," added Bnr.

They left the next day.

The Universal Portal System deposited the two of them onto a subway platform in New York City. After they each instantaneously shape-shifted to resemble humans (Abr wearing kakis and a pink polo shirt and Bnr dressed in skinny jeans and black tee-shirt), they followed the crowd up a long escalator to street level, right in the heart of Manhattan. Immediately they noticed something odd; some people were wearing face mask coverings and others weren't.

Abr whispered to Bnr, "What's going on?"

Bnr sniffed. "Maybe it's because the air smells so bad."

Abr held his nose and nodded. "Probably, but I'm going to find out for sure." He put out his arm and stopped a young man sauntering by carrying a skateboard. "Excuse me. Could you please tell us why some people are wearing those things on their face?"

The young man had dreadlocks and wore a red tee-shirt and baggy pants. He gave them a perplexed look. "You mean masks? Haven't you heard about the pandemic?"

Neither of them had a clue but Bnr was quick to play along. "A little, but tell us what you know."

"Okay," he said, agreeably. "It began in China in 2019 and spread around the world from there. It got bad here in the States in March of 2020 and has stayed bad ever since."

"Wow!" Bnr exclaimed. "That's about…"

"Yeah, it's been over two years, now. Wearing a mask has helped slow the spread of the virus."

Abr asked, "Why doesn't everyone wear one?"

The young man shrugged, flipped his dreadlocks back onto his shoulder and said, "Because they're idiots." He put down his skateboard, stepped on and skated off down the sidewalk.

Abr and Bnr watched him weave in and out of the crowd.

"We should get masks," Abr said. "To be on the safe side."

"Yes, we should," Bnr agreed. "And to fit in. Say, I have an idea. Let's try an experiment."

"What do you have in mind?"

"Why don't you wear a mask and I won't. We'll see if it makes a difference."

"Sounds good," Abr said. "I'd like a black one like the guy we talked to had."

"Great," Bnr said. "Let's go get you one."

One year later, Bnr, the non-mask wearing alien, returned alone to Zerros. After he completed his initial de-briefing, the supreme commander summoned him. "What happened? Why'd you come back alone? Did Abr die even though he was wearing one of those ridiculous masks?" He laughed. "Abr was always kind of a gullible sort."

"No," Bnr was quick to respond. "The mask helped him a lot. He never got sick." Then he grinned sheepishly. "On the other hand, I got the virus and almost died. It was touch and go for a while, but," he pointed to himself, "as you can see, I made it back just fine."

Knx was unimpressed. "Whatever… Getting back to Abr, if he's not dead, why didn't he come back with you?"

"You'll never believe it, sir."

"What?"

Bnr grinned. "He met a lady."

"Impossible. You scientists aren't supposed fall for that kind of nonsense. You're all about the science. Research. Facts. Testing and more testing. You don't have time for romance."

Bnr grinned even more. "Never-the-less, sir, that's what

happened. 'Hook, line and sinker' is the expression they use on earth. 'The whole kit-and-caboodle'. 'The…' "

"All right! I get your drift."

"He's in love, sir."

"What! What kind of stupid thing is that to say? Love. It's a bunch of…" Knx was beside himself, not one inclined toward anything to do with amorous intentions. "It's a bunch of crap, that's what it is."

"He's really smitten, sir. It's pretty emotional for him, too, and he's not used to dealing with feelings."

"I should say not."

"And it's complicated."

"How so?" The supreme commander was on shaky ground when it came to talking about love.

"Well, she's brilliant. She stands in the harbour of New York City and is kind of a beacon for liberty. She's got a lot of responsibility."

"I can imagine."

"Yes. She's made of metal and Abr adores her. He's with her all the time taking care of her, cleaning her and watching out for her. She doesn't move much. Plus, she's kind of quiet, but he enjoys talking to her even if she doesn't talk back. Like I said, he's very smitten."

"Even with this pandemic going on he's not worried about getting sick?"

"No, sir. He wears his mask. He's being safe. He's very happy."

Knx was quiet for a moment. Then he sighed, giving Abr up as a lost cause, and focused on Bnr. "Okay, then. What about the mission to take over the planet? You were there for a year. Should we attack now?"

"No, sir. I'd wait. The pandemic will kill many more people, especially if they persist in not following the guidelines. It's inevitable. After that happens it'll make dealing with them that much easier. Fewer people to worry about."

"That makes sense."

"Thank you, sir." Bnr was quiet for a moment and then added. "Sir, if you don't mind. I have an idea."

"About what?"

Speeding along the takeover."

Knx was not a patient man. "Get to the point, Bnr."

"Well, sir, I looked into getting a job at one of the pharmaceutical companies that's working on making a vaccine."

Knx was intrigued. "Yes?"

"You know with my credentials I'm a very good scientist, right?"

"The point, Bnr."

"Well, I've done a bit of research. I can make the vaccine look like it will work, but, in reality, it won't work. People will be excited to take the vaccine, but it won't help them. More people will die and it'll throw the world into chaos."

"You sure you can do that?"

"Piece-of-cake, sir," to use an expression on earth.

Knx grimaced. "They sound like an odd bunch."

"They are, sir. Extremely."

"So, you get a job with a pharmaceutical company and mess up the vaccine. Right?

"Yes."

"The pandemic goes on and people keep dying because the vaccine doesn't work.

"Yes, sir. And chaos ensures."

"And the takeover is easier. It's brilliant, Bnr."

"Thank you, sir."

Knx was silent, grinning, thinking about adding another planet to his collect. Life was good.

"Um, sir?" Bnr asked.

"What?"

"When do you want me to leave?"

"As soon as possible."

"I'll go tomorrow."

"Good." Bnr stood to leave. "Oh, and, Bnr."

"What, sir?"

"Don't get hung up doing what Abr is doing."
"Oh, I won't. It's not good science."
Knx smiled. He was liking Bnr more and more.

Shadowlands

Susan A Eames

The light drained from the sky like someone opening a vein. Trees blackened as if they'd been charred. Our world turned monochrome. I stood looking out of the cabin window and shivered.

We had fled the city into the shadowlands with little more than the clothes on our backs and our precious supply of vaccine. Since the breakdown of the government, the looters had turned the city into a war zone.

Robbie's mountain cabin seemed like our only option. But although I was grateful that we had a safe haven, the cabin was depressingly basic.

"No electricity?" I said with a frown.

"No, Mags," Robbie said.

"And no running water either?"

"No, we'll have to collect water in buckets from the stream."

"Christ."

"You'll get used to it."

"I know, but…"

"The way I see it, the best way to survive is if we keep a low profile. That means keeping things simple. Be thankful you have a roof over your head, Mags."

I turned back to the window.

Robbie lit an oil lamp, casting long shadows in the room. He came up behind me, massaged my shoulders and dropped a kiss on the back of my neck.

I could see movement in the undergrowth. "Something's out there."

Robbie sighed. "City Girl, it's just the wind."

The night thickened with cold. I shivered again.

"They got bears hereabouts?" I asked.

Robbie huffed in exasperation. "You crazy?"

"Well, it looks like bear country."

He gave me a look. “We need firewood.” He went outside.

I felt cross and guilty in equal measure. Robbie was doing his best. We were in this together and I should be pulling my weight instead of acting like a spoilt brat.

Minutes passed. How long did it take to gather up some firewood? I cracked open the door. “Robbie?”

I heard a muffled thump over by the woodpile and suddenly felt an indelible dread.

“Robbie? Are you messing with me?”

I heard saw-toothed voices.

“Robbie?” I whispered.

A barnacled shadow moved on the edge of vision. I slammed the door shut, fumbling for the bolts. Heavy footsteps on the deck stilled my panicked fingers.

I stared at the door, waiting.

~~~~~~~~
~~~~~~~~

The Authors

Endings, I think, in life as in fiction, carry us, with all that has gone before, into the land between one story and the next.

Sally Angell

Glance back and reminisce… then stare hope in the face and accept its gifts, for the most beautiful new dawns arise from the darkest and deepest of nights.

Angela Elizabeth Armstrong

I hope we'll remember the importance of kindness.

Cath Barton
Writer

May the horror of the pandemic remind us all to appreciate each and every moment of our lives what we have and to never forget what was lost.

Jim Bates

I came of age.

As a London Bulge child (those born 1946-50) I could not understand why so many family conversations were prefaced with 'before the war' and 'during the war' and seemed always more important than anything happening in my little post-war world of planting my garden, singing and playing the piano.

Now I do understand and even the gardening and the music have shown their importance in the historical British cycle of 'bugger on, we are all in this together', to recount to future generations.

Margaret Bulleyment
Retired teacher and writer

The Best Things in Life are Free (or are they?) – When I originally wrote this story, little did I know it would be that literally the best things in life, (freedom and oxygen) would be eroded!

In my flash story for *Aftermath*, I have added an evil character who has abused our freedoms for monetary gain and who is able to use his power to hide the truth.

Lynn Clement

The 'Roaring Twenties' followed the 1918 Pandemic. People who feared life outside their homes suddenly found themselves revelling in their renewed freedom with herd immunity. We long for that day.

Dawn DeBraal

'This too shall pass' has become my mantra when things get tough.

Tony Domaille

The Covid 19 pandemic has enabled me to learn how to embrace solitude and cherish companionship in all its forms.

Susan A Eames
Travel and fiction writer

Lockdown has made me stiller, more anxious but also more thankful. The small things mean more.

Alyson Faye

Finding beauty on my doorstep and realising it's always been there has been my greatest discovery and the greatest gift during lock down.

Nicole Fitton
Fiction writer and doorstep explorer

Every experience is a story; an adventure, a quest for light beyond the darkness. We are all a part of the narrative of time that says whatever can be must be better than what now is. So we strive and yearn as we live and tell the tale of years, hoping for hope beyond hope, longing for light and joy. And I say with those who have been and those yet to come: "I laugh… I live… I love!"

John Guest
Metaphysician, storyteller, disciple

It’s made me extra conscious of how fortunate I am to be an introvert, living in a wealthy country in the age of the Internet.

Anne Goodwin

Author of fiction from novels to flash

Little chinks of light and knowing that other people were not too far away have been a comfort and a support over the past months.

Vanessa Horn

The one thing I am not looking forward to after the restrictions are lifted is that feeling of not wanting to miss out on anything, which results in having to do everything.

Janet Howson

A plague sent by God? Nature getting its own back on this problematic species? Plague and pestilence getting the upper hand in their struggle with animal life on the planet? A push for us to embrace the IT revolution? An opportunity for bringing out the best in humanity? And suppressing the worst? How are we doing?

Gill James

After shielding in lockdown I experienced kindness like never before. Long may our humanity overcome the challenges in our future.

Amanda Jones

When we look back, we’ll marvel at mankind’s creativity and ingenuity and the advancements in science and technology. I wonder if we’ll be as impressed with mankind’s behaviour? Time will tell.

Dawn Knox

Writer, hoping to be impressed, fearing the worst.

It seems that we’ve been living in an alternate universe for the past year.

Henry Lewi

I am thankful for good friends.

Madeleine McDonald
Writer, editor

We have been
dormant yet growing,
locked down but preparing,
attacked and surviving.
There will be
freedom and flight.

Linda Morse

Whatever befalls us, try to laugh. If you cannot do that, then smile.

Roger Noons

The lockdown has taught us to be still and by ourselves, which I think is vital for personal growth and self-awareness.

Brigita Orel
Writer and translator

My heart beats with gratitude for all the people risking their own health to make our world safe again.

Clarissa Pattern
Eternal dreamer

A writer is never lonely, all those characters wanting to talk, act, develop. Life's cast of friends, enemies, and lovers all wanting your attention to appear on the page.

Colin Payn

Still contemplating the 'long tail' of the Aftermath.

Mari Phillips

I know what aftermath is. I have seen it. It is new for me. It gives me hope.

Pam Pottinger

There was good that came from the pandemic and hopefully we will carry those lessons forward and never forget.

Niles Reddick

We crawl through 2021 and discover pieces of hope, sanity, and toilet paper.

Hannah Retallick
Writer, editor

I discovered the importance of seeing my workmates first thing in our day – only electronically. But those little chats you have first thing before starting the day are priceless.

C L Spillard

Germination follows the bleak just as surely as sunshine follows the rain.

Dianne Stadhams

During this time, we've been given a chance to learn and appreciate that our relationships – however short or long they may be – are indeed blessings beyond measure.

Ray Suchow

The future: where things will not be quite as they were before.

P. A. Westgate

Looking ahead to a new dawn of heightened perceptions of both humanity and also the humanities. Hopefully, a brighter light.

Anne Wilson
Fiction writer.

I sincerely hope that the light at the end of the tunnel is real and not imagined.

Robin Wrigley

www.ingramcontent.com/pod-product-compliance
Lightning Source LLC
LaVergne TN
LVHW010945100826
845153LV00002B/142

* 9 7 8 1 9 1 0 5 4 2 7 4 3 *